SEQUOIA
SCOUT

SEQUOIA SCOUT

★ ★ ★

BROCK & BODIE THOENE

BETHANY HOUSE PUBLISHERS
MINNEAPOLIS, MINNESOTA 55438

Cover illustration by Dan Thornberg,
Bethany House Publishers staff artist.

Published by Bethany House Publishers
A Ministry of Bethany Fellowship, Inc.
6820 Auto Club Road, Minneapolis, Minnesota 55438

Printed in the United States of America

Library of Congress Cataloging-in-Publication Data

Thoene, Brock, 1952–
    Sequoia scout / by Brock and Bodie Thoene.
       p. cm. — (Saga of the Sierras)

    1. California—History—To 1846—Fiction.
2. Yokuts Indians—Fiction. I. Thoene, Bodie, 1951–   .
II. Title. III. Series: Thoene, Brock, 1952–   Saga of the Sierras.
PS3570.H463S24   1991
813'.54—dc20   91–25366
ISBN 1–55661–165–X (pbk.)   CIP

"For Penny and Woody Watson,
with blessings and thanks . . ."

Books by Brock and Bodie Thoene

The Zion Covenant

Vienna Prelude
Prague Counterpoint
Munich Signature
Jerusalem Interlude
Danzig Passage
Warsaw Requiem

The Zion Chronicles

The Gates of Zion
A Daughter of Zion
The Return to Zion
A Light in Zion
The Key to Zion

The Shiloh Legacy

In My Father's House
A Thousand Shall Fall
Say to This Mountain

Saga of the Sierras

The Man From Shadow Ridge
Riders of the Silver Rim
Gold Rush Prodigal
Sequoia Scout
Cannons of the Comstock
The Year of the Grizzly
Shooting Star

Non-Fiction

Protecting Your Income and Your Family's Future
Writer to Writer

BROCK AND BODIE THOENE have combined their skills to become a prolific writing team. Bodie's award-winning writing of THE ZION CHRONICLES and THE ZION COVENANT series is supported by Brock's careful research and development. Co-authors of SAGA OF THE SIERRAS, this husband and wife team has spent years researching the history and the drama of the Old West.

Their work has been acclaimed by men such as John Wayne and Louis L'Amour. With their children, Brock and Bodie live in the Sierras, giving firsthand authenticity to settings and descriptions in this frontier series.

CHAPTER 1

When Will Reed came to his senses, he looked up into the low ceiling of the tiny brush shelter and knew immediately where he was. But when he tried to leap to his feet, he discovered that both his hands and legs were bound with rawhide thongs. His lunge upward accomplished only a clumsy lurch, and he fell face forward on another man.

"Get off me," screamed Aubrey, "my leg's broke!"

Outside the hut, the rhythmic chanting of the Mojave Indians was accompanied by eerie dry clicking of gourds and punctuated by increasingly wild yells.

Will rolled off Aubrey as gently as he could and came to rest face up beside Forchet who was still unconscious. The Frenchman's breathing was ragged, and a raspy gurgle brought to memory the arrow that penetrated Forchet's chest just before a club had crashed into the back of Will's head and everything went black.

Aubrey, nearly hysterical, sobbed and repeated over and over again, "I don't want to die . . . don't kill me . . . I don't want to die . . ."

No help there, Will decided. He forced himself to think rationally about the spot they were in, what he knew about the terrain and the possibilities for escape. His heart pounded faster as the rhythm of the gourd-accompanied chants gained in tempo. Aubrey changed his moan to, "They skin folks alive. They're gonna peel us. . . . Why can't they just kill us and be done with it? Why'd I ever come on this trip?"

Outside, another yell went up from the dancers as more brush was thrown on the fire, blazing up instantly in a thunderous roar. With the sound, Will wondered if the Mojaves intended to set fire to the brush shelter that served as their prison cell. Aubrey could be wasting his breath fretting about being flayed; roasted alive might be their sudden fate.

Forchet stirred momentarily and rolled half over on his side. The light from the brush fire outside illuminated the open flap of his buckskin shirt. Under the shirt, tucked in a leather strap that Forchet wore over one shoulder was the concealed sheath of a skinning knife. Had the Indians searched the French trapper and found the knife?

Will's glance flew toward the uprooted creosote bush that served as the doorway. No movement there yet. He heaved himself up to a sitting position, frightening Aubrey.

"What—what are you doing?"

"Shh!" Will hissed.

He scooted over toward the unconscious Frenchman by bunching his heels up under him and thrusting himself across the small rocky space. Two pushes and he was sitting upright beside Forchet's chest.

"What is it?" inquired Aubrey again, loudly.

Will shook his head angrily from side to side, silencing Aubrey, then gesturing with a jerk of his chin toward the barely visible knife handle.

Aubrey raised up on one elbow and his bushy eyebrows rose almost to the level of his hair. Like a fool he made as if to stand, then his face contorted with pain and he shrank back with a groan. He waved his bound hands toward his injured leg.

Will nodded grimly, then attempted to lean down sideways to reach the knife handle with his fingertips. Halfway down he over-balanced and fell onto Forchet.

There! Will's fingers just brushed the wooden handle of the skinning knife. The rawhide straps cut deeply into his skin as he tried to spread his tightly wrapped wrists. He could barely force his fingers far enough apart to grasp the handle. Only the last joint of two fingers had any purchase on the rounded wooden end.

Then from outside came a sudden glare, a crackling roar and a chorus of shrill howls as more brush was thrown on the fire. Will's attention was torn away from his goal. The end of the knife squirted from between his numb fingers.

Doggedly he set to work again, fixing all his concentration on the task of grasping the knife. He pulled it up toward Forchet's chin with a steady, tense draw, afraid that a sudden jerk would loosen his grip. Beads of sweat stood out on his forehead, gathering into large drops that rolled down into his green eyes.

Forchet stirred and heaved a deep sigh, rustling his coal black beard. To Will's horror the wounded trapper began to roll back again, carrying the precious tool away from his reach.

Every muscle in Will's body tensed, and his toes curled inside the leather moccasins he wore. He dared not yank or twist. He could only hang on desperately with his fingertips as Forchet completed a slow turn away, the motion of his body drawing the weapon from its sheath.

Will stared in stunned disbelief at the initials *GR* engraved on the blade. Flickers of light from the fire glinted on the steel. He pivoted slowly back upright, clutching the Green River skinning knife. The heavy blade came to rest on the topmost strap that bound his hands. Before attempting to saw at the rawhide strands, he threw a triumphant look toward Aubrey.

Aubrey had been holding his breath and clenching his teeth against the pain in his leg. His fears about the Mojaves' intentions were reflected in his terrified expression. By the dim light that penetrated the brush pile enclosing them, Aubrey could see the blade and the flash of a victory smile from Will.

Aubrey's pent-up breath exploded with a rush, "You've got it!"

At that instant there was an emphatic clap of hands to gourd drums and a resounding stamp of Mojave feet as their dance abruptly ended.

Aubrey regarded Will with wide-eyed apprehension. Had the Indians heard Aubrey's exclamation? Or did the sudden stop of the dancing and chanting mean that they were coming for the white men? Was it too late?

Then just as suddenly as the ceremony had ended, another one began. The pounding and shaking of the rattles resumed, and so did the chanting.

Both trappers sighed their relief, and Will grimly set to work sawing the leather thongs. Now the tightness of the bindings helped as he was able to steady the blade downward against them. Will blessed Forchet's attention to his equipment: The recently sharpened edge began to bite on the rawhide, although Will could only work it a fraction of an inch at a time with his fingertips.

Scarcely two minutes went by, but their passage seemed like hours. Finally the rawhide strip snapped apart. He was left with a loop still tied around each wrist and a length hanging down. But his hands were free. With one slash of the knife, his feet were loose as well.

He could see the pleading in Aubrey's eyes.

"Don't worry," he whispered into Aubrey's ear, "I won't leave you behind, or Forchet either. If the raft is still on the bank where they jumped us, we'll ride the river out of here."

Will cut through the thongs on Aubrey's arms even before he finished speaking. But he was afraid to meet Aubrey's eyes. Will knew that the chances of eluding recapture while trying to move an unconscious man and a cripple past half-a-hundred Indians were almost non-existent. But he couldn't chance Aubrey starting into his moaning despair again. At least this way they could go down fighting, so he said no more.

Aubrey's bound hands sprang apart with an audible twang. Looking for a place to break out, Will turned his attention to the heap of brush that formed the back wall of their cell. He needed a spot that he could drag the other two men through without signaling their escape by too much rustling and shaking of the hut.

He spotted an arch in the yucca-palm branches that afforded an opening near the ground. The space was plugged with a clump of mesquite, which could be easily pushed out. Holding the knife at the ready, Will plunged headfirst into the brush, breaking out of the makeshift prison. With the hut shielding him from the fire, the deeper darkness beyond called him to save himself. Instead, he cleared the mesquite from the hole and prepared to rescue his compatriots.

Back into the hut he went, mentally urging Aubrey to be ready. Every second was precious.

He saw Aubrey's arms reaching out toward him, eager to be pulled to safety. Will stretched out his free hand, his fingertips finding Aubrey's trembling grasp.Aubrey had just locked his grip on Will's wrists when the brush doorway in front of the hut was pulled aside. A shaft of light from the Indian bonfire blinded both men.

Will sprang forward in a rush. His right hand pushed the knife point toward the intruder in a savage thrust, but he was off balance with his lunge and his vision was dazzled by the light. Instead of striking home, the blow was knocked aside. A forearm as lean and hard as a dried mesquite limb crashed into the side of his head, staggering him. Two dark hands as strong as steel traps closed over his wrists and shook the knife from his grip.

Will was on his knees, expecting the next instant to be his last. But the knife slash did not follow.

Instead, his assailant turned back to the doorway of the cell and rapidly pulled the brush shut. Will waited in the darkness to see what would happen next. He could not make out the features of the strong intruder, but the man was an Indian.

Will's eyes adjusted to the darkness again, and he could see the attacker kneeling and facing him only a couple feet away. The Indian spoke in a low but audible tone, and his words were in English.

"You must keep still. My name is Mangas. I am Apache. I tried to tell the Mojaves that you were not Spanish and to not attack you, but they would not listen.

"I have convinced two of the old chiefs to let you go,

but the young warrior men will not listen. I cannot save you all, but if one of you will lead the war party away, I will put the other two safely on the river."

Even though the chanting and dancing outside continued unabated, the stillness inside the prison was suddenly absolute.

In a moment Will spoke. "It was up to me before, and I guess it still is now. How much time have I got, Mangas?"

"A few minutes only. You must hurry. I will try to put them on the wrong trail—this is all I can do."

"All right then, I'm ready." Will grasped Aubrey's hand. "Good luck. Take care of Frenchy as best you're able."

Mangas handed Will the skinning knife. Will accepted the weapon, then shook the Indian's hand and stared into his eyes. "Someday maybe I'll get to hear why you're doing this, but for now, thanks."

"Go with God," replied the Apache, and Will turned and dove through the opening and into the inky night of the Mojave desert.

Will crawled swiftly over the brush at the back of the Mojave camp. He had heard that these Mojaves drank a fermented brew made from cactus. He fervently hoped that they had been soaking in it this night.

Plunging through a screen of creosote bushes, he rolled down an embankment into a ravine and came up desperately clutching the knife. Shaking sand from his ears, he strained to hear a change in the sounds of the camp. Still no cry of pursuit.

Which way to run? he wondered. *The sand either direction along the river will leave too good a trail, so it's cross-country for me.*

He scrambled up the other side of the draw, then glanced over his shoulder at the glare of the fire. *Straight away from that is as good as any.*

Will climbed a sandstone bluff and stood just below its crest so as to not be skylined against the night. He was on the opposite side of the river from the trail he and the other trappers had been following when they were captured. The Indians had taken everything but the Frenchman's knife. Now Will was alone in the desert without map or compass, without food, and headed away from the only certain source of water.

A sudden clamor from the camp behind him replaced the chanting with cries of anger and outrage. From the bluff Will could see sparks rush outward from the glow of the fire as warriors grabbed flaming branches and began a hurried search of the camp.

Will watched just long enough to see the sparks gather together again in a body and race upstream along the river bank. *Good,* he thought. *This Mangas fellow knows his business. He's sent them away from me and away from the direction of the raft at the same time.*

Will remembered hearing Beckwith describe the land west of the river as flat plains, brushy and dry, rising slowly to meet the eastern slope of the Sierras.

He frowned as he remembered that tonight Beckwith was floating face down in the river with his skin full of arrows.

And unless I find some way to get off this plain by day-break, that's what I'll look like. Come first light I'll stand out like a black cat on a snowbank.

For the next two hours he loped over the brush plain with the silent, ground-covering trot of a coyote, whose presence in the desert could be told from the barks and yips heard in the night.

Fixing his sight on the North Star, he kept it on his right shoulder as he ran. He heard the angry buzz of a rattlesnake's warning, but he never saw the reptile as he raced on into the night.

Pressing his elbows tightly into his aching sides, he forced himself to keep going. The Mojaves would be on his trail by now. At best he figured he had an hour's start on them, and within an hour it would be daylight.

Ahead lay his only hope: Though yet unseen, he believed a line of the Sierras reared themselves not too far to the west. Will's long legs had tramped many miles from his uncle's Vicksburg home, but they had never been called on for such an effort as this. Travel at night made it difficult to judge distances, but Will figured he had covered fifteen miles or so when the sky behind him began to noticeably lighten.

He threw nervous glances back the way he had come. Whenever he could, Will directed his path over rocky surfaces that would leave less trace of his passing, but finding a place to hide before full daylight was his main concern. Fortunately, a rising east wind was blowing dust over his tracks almost as soon as he made them.

There were precious few spots that offered any chance of concealment. The scrubby creosote brush was not over three feet high. In the thickest places it formed clumps big enough for a man to lie down in, but if he let himself get surrounded, the Mojaves would search an ever-decreasing circle till he was again their prisoner.

From the high mountain plateau, the old Indian's gaze lingered on the distant horizon. At the extreme edge of his vision flickered an orange star that pulsed and flared in time to an unheard rhythm.

He hunched his shoulders deeper into the rabbitskin cloak. An involuntary shiver reminded him of a nearby responsibility, and the old man bent over the sleeping form of a child.

The deeply etched lines on the weathered cheeks softened for an instant as he tugged another blanket of rabbit fur up around the boy. A drowsy, eight-year-old voice murmured, "Is it morning already, Grandfather?"

"No," replied the elder. "It is still some time yet before dawn. Sleep," he instructed.

Perversely, the mounded heap of rabbitskin and child stirred and sat up. "But why are you awake, Grandfather?"

"I keep watch, boy," replied the old man. "But now, since you are awake, look there."

The orange glow which the ancient eyes turned toward was no longer alone in the dark line which separated desert sand from desert sky. Both the young eyes and the old saw the flare multiply into many, as if the low star was dripping a cascade of sparks.

A deep, guttural sound came from the man, in words the boy did not catch.

"What did you say, Grandfather? What are those lights?"

For a time of silence which the child respected there was no reply. Then Grandfather spoke in measured tones, "There is evil about tonight, and you see its dance."

"But the bright lights are pretty," protested the boy. "They fly around like sparks from our campfires. Where is our campfire, Grandfather?"

"Hush now," urged the ancient voice with a hint of

impatience. "These flickers hide wickedness behind their bright show. We have no fire because we do not want to attract such moths to our flame. Lights such as those are always ready to snuff . . ." The old man broke off his answer because his listener had gone back to sleep as abruptly as he had awakened.

Crouched down on a rocky ledge high above the desert sweep, the elder Indian studied the glints of flame rushing about. The pinpoints were slowly drawing closer to the mountains on which he and the child rested, and he dreaded to see them come. The east wind seemed to propel them along.

He watched until the finest thread of pale blue touched the eastern-most rim of the bowl of night. As the dawn spread its gray hand, it pushed back the dark, so that the sparks dimmed and faded. But in each place, just as he had warned, Grandfather watched each light be replaced by a form of blackness, scurrying over the land.

Suddenly his eyes found what he had been seeking. At the near rim of the desert floor, appearing almost beneath his feet near a Joshua tree, was a lone dark insect-creature. It moved in a purposeful rush, seeming to look for a place to hide before the fast approaching light of day.

Grandfather stood once more. The surging wind was in his face, just as the rays of the sun glinted into his narrowed eyes. *Hurry*, he whispered urgently, without saying to whom he spoke.

The wind acted as if it had heard him, and obligingly raised its tempo. From the east flowed an airborne river of dust. Wispy at first, like smoke, the blowing sand soon formed a dagger-strike of black that competed with the sun for possession of the land.

The dust cloud knifed across the desert, blotting out the further horizon. It next overshadowed some of the black figures that had fallen behind the others. The partition of swirling dirt extended itself upward from the ground like a curtain that concealed by being pulled up instead of lowered.

The cloud of sand passed between pursued and pursuers. As Grandfather watched from his perch high above the scene, an enormous convulsion of the dust storm enveloped even the lone figure at the very base of the mountain.

"Good," Grandfather nodded in approval. Then, "Come, boy," he urged the sleeping child. "Day is here."

The change in elevation had grown more acute. From the flat plain nearer the river, the land now had a noticeable rake to it. The increased pressure on Will's legs took a toll on his lungs and strength, slowing his pace. More than once he was thankful for the breeze that pushed him from behind. He passed more Joshua trees, their contorted shapes looking in the early light like tortured men frozen in moments of great torment.

His guiding star was gone, but in its place the elongated shadows of the trees pointed him on toward the west. Ahead, the glimmering rays of the sun were just touching the highest peaks of the southern Sierra Nevadas. But Will did not see the arriving day as friendly. The spreading glow that already sharpened the images of trees and rocks threatened to pin his dark form against the dusty gray landscape. Should he halt his march, Will knew a Mojave spear would complete the work the sun's rays had begun.

He set his course toward the tallest tree on the horizon. Will saw that the rise in the desert floor broke sharply against a line of cliffs. No relief in that change of elevation, the cliffs were sheer. Slick rock faces of sandstone offered no handholds. He was running into a horseshoe-shaped rim of rock, but no direction in view offered any more hope of escape than another.

Panting, he stumbled on over the uneven ground, aimed toward the shadow cast by the tallest Joshua as it flowed up and into the cliffs.

This remnant of night shadow appeared unnaturally elongated, even though produced by a tall tree. The shadow stood out against the pale sandstone wall as if made of some darker, coarser material.

As he passed the tree, Will threw another glance over his shoulder. Far behind him on a distant ridge he could make out dark moving dots, the pinpoints of torchlight flickering out against the morning glare of the sun. Racing on, he pushed his burning legs for more speed. Gasping the dry desert air in great gulps, his throat felt like a parched corn stalk planted in the middle of his chest.

When he reached the sandstone wall, there was nowhere left to run. An unbroken wall of unclimbable rock stretched both ways from Will's perch in the shadow of the Joshua tree's limbs. His pursuers moved relentlessly nearer.

There was a crack in the rock face behind Will, but nowhere was it wider than a handbreadth. As the sun climbed above the desert, the protecting shadow of the tree began to shrink. Will leaned against the rock. For the first time all night, he faced the wind and gravel as it pelted his cheeks. In between breaths he prayed for a way out, prayed that all his efforts had not been wasted, that somehow, someway there was a way of escape.

And then, as if in answer to his desperate prayer, the veil of dust and sand howled into a blinding storm, drawing a thick dark curtain between Will and his pursuers.

Ten years of trapping had brought him to this moment. Ten years in search of fortune. Ten years since the mountain men had come east to the trading post of his uncle with their stories of the high lonesome—stories that had caused the young Will Reed to lie awake at night and dream.

He had been a young colt when he left Vicksburg, lean, gawky, but full of promise. The years had added bone, muscle strength and the sinew of endurance. Two dozen trips west with men like Jedidiah Smith and Jim Bridger had given him wisdom in the ways of the harsh and beautiful land. Two years among the Cherokees had made him more Indian than some Indians.

Will had never returned to Vicksburg, though he had never made his fortune or found his promised land. The restless spirit his uncle had cursed had brought him to this moment when all that separated him from death was a shifting curtain of sand.

He covered his face with his red kerchief and pulled his buckskin coat close around him. Turning his back to the wind, he let the hide clothing bear the brunt of the stinging grit. Like a lean brush wolf, he curled his body into a crease of the rock face and hoped that the storm that had saved him would not now suck the breath from his burning lungs.

CHAPTER 2

The east wind swirled dust around the feet of Don Jose Dominguez as he stood in the hall of his hacienda. He stared at it morosely, then stomped his boots as if he could scare the dust away like he would a mouse.

He had forgotten that his new boots were too small even on his rather small feet. Stomping sent a wave of pain through already pinched toes. Characteristically, Dominguez swore at the bootmaker, but would not stoop to remove the offending articles. He also swore at his Indian housekeeper, although the dirt now dancing in the air around his head had come into the hallway when he pitched his filthy chapedero leggings onto the tile floor.

The picture of Dominguez's overstuffed body perched atop his tiny feet mirrored the relationship between his ambition and the quality of his soul: one was far too ponderously inflated to be supported well by the small stature of the other.

Dominguez, a bad soldier and a worse officer, was quick to take credit and unable to stand blame. But he had somehow managed to live to retirement. A threat to expose the misdeeds of a relative of higher rank had obtained him a pension in the form of a land grant. The relative, acutely aware of what an embarrassment Don

Jose was likely to be, made sure that the rancho being offered was far away, near the dusty presidio of Santa Barbara.

Dominguez proceeded to make life as miserable for his ranch hands as he had for his troops. When the Indians he hired from the mission ran away, it was because they were "shiftless renegades," not because he disciplined them harshly for the smallest infraction. And if they refused to work the hours he demanded, it was because they were lazy, not because he fed them only two scanty helpings of beans and barley a day.

His cattle did not thrive because his land was not the best and there was certainly not enough of it. He whipped a vaquero until the man could not stand for suggesting that he might be overgrazing. It was the subject of land and how much he did not have that drove Don Jose Dominguez into his most frequent diatribe.

"It is the law!" stormed Dominguez. "It was supposed to happen ten years ago and more. Governor Figueroa is a weakling and a fool."

"Calm yourself, my son," soothed the short priest, Father Quintana. "Figueroa is a good Catholic and respects the church—"

"Figueroa is supposed to uphold the law. And the law says the missions are to be secularized and the land turned over to the Indians."

"But the heads of my order do not believe that the neophytes are ready to manage their own land," argued the priest.

This last comment brought a snort of derision from the bull-like nostrils of Dominguez. His barrel chest swung around with such momentum that the little father flinched in fear of being knocked over.

"Of course they cannot manage their affairs. The mission lands should belong to us, the soldiers who fought for it. So should the mission Indians. We need them to work the land." Dominguez's eyes narrowed and he peered down at the priest with suspicion. "Whose side are you on, Father?"

"Yours of course, I assure you," pledged Quintana, his open hands raised to placate the Don's anger. "There is a time coming when the church's lands will be forfeited to the state and redistributed, and I . . ." his voice died away.

The burly ranchero was without mercy and completed the sentence for the priest. "And you want to make certain that you are in line to receive some. Isn't that right, Quintana?"

"My order is headed by fine men. But they would actually *insist* on giving all the land to the Indians. Can you imagine? I would become a parish priest, living on the donations of dirty farmers."

"Instead of being a ranchero with a fine home and hundreds of Indios working for you." The thickset Dominguez turned on his thin legs, back toward the window overlooking his front pasture. "And I will be the leader I should be," he observed. Behind him Quintana obediently bobbed his head. "Instead of six thousand acres I should own ten, no twenty . . . even a hundred as much," Dominguez said. "And in the meantime, we will continue to supplement our income, eh, Quintana?" taunted the ranchero.

The little priest stiffened. He had buried much of his conscience, but he hated the reminder of how far he had fallen from his supposed role as pastor and shepherd to the flock of the mission Indians.

"We only ship off to the Sonoran mines those neophytes who prove to be renegades—the ones without remorse for their backsliding or chronic running away," the priest protested.

"And if we encourage their rebellious ways, or 'accidentally' capture a few wild Indios along with the runaways," Dominguez needled, "well, it is just 'God's will.' Isn't that right, Quintana?"

"I have seen no laws being broken," said the gray-robed friar primly.

"Bah! You are blind at very convenient times! A hypocrite of the first water!"

———

For three days the warm Santa Ana wind had blown from the east and swept across the foothills of Santa Barbara.

Francesca Rivera y Cruz locked the louvered doors of her balcony and blamed her restlessness on that wind.

"It will wither the wild flowers before they have a chance to grow," she had complained to her father over breakfast just this morning.

Her brother Ricardo accused her of not caring for the health of the flowers at all. "You only care that the schooner of that pirate Billy Easton won't be able to come into the harbor in such a wind. Admit it, Francesca," he teased. "Bolts of cloth and lace handkerchiefs are the reason for your impatience with the Santa Ana."

Perhaps Ricardo is right, she mused when the winds had finally shifted and a cool ocean breeze wafted in from the west.

Throwing open her shutters, she stepped out onto her balcony and breathed deeply of the sweet cool air. The schooner of trader Easton had been spotted off the coast and would no doubt be making anchor in this gentle breeze. But this assurance did not drive away the restlessness in her heart.

She pulled the comb from her shining black hair and let it tumble down over her shoulders. The fingers of the sea breeze touched her face softly and she closed her eyes. What was it, this restlessness? Not the desire for a new dress or a few yards of fabric! What did that matter when there was no man she cared to impress?

White clouds scudded across the bright California sky. In the distance she could see the sea birds playing on the currents of wind. Those familiar sights did not give her peace. She felt the presence of *something* very near. *Nameless and frightening!* Like nothing she'd ever felt before. Yet she longed to learn the name of this fear and know its face.

A whisper of things to come had blown in on the Santa Ana wind and stirred her heart with the warning that nothing would ever be the same.

––––––––

Captain Alfredo Zuniga believed in his natural superiority. He was born to command, to be recognized as a leader of men. He had been a junior officer in Santa Fe, New Mexico, when Manuel Armijo was the governor of that province.

Zuniga emulated Armijo, who was fond of remarking that "God rules the heavens and Armijo rules the earth." The young officer rapidly gained a reputation as a brave and ruthless Indian fighter.

If Zuniga was admired by his subordinates, he was also feared by them. He had the eyes of a shark; lifeless and deadly. With a small man's resentment of larger statures, he lost no opportunity to prove his superiority by the code "duello."

Zuniga killed men for slight or imagined offenses. He thought nothing of manufacturing offenses to eliminate rivals. One saber duel that ended another man's life was over a bad debt that Zuniga did not intend to pay. On another occasion he had skewered a man in order to possess his woman.

Most soldiers considered California to be a backwater, a dead-end posting, but Zuniga had requested the assignment to Presidio Santa Barbara. Civilized society did not tolerate the likes of Captain Zuniga, and he knew it. He found his heart's desire: a location where he was the only law, accountable to no one but himself.

He had no regard for anything except superior force. It was his way with enemies and women alike. And if he could project a cool detachment, it was only while gauging the opponent's strength, probing for the weakness which was always present somewhere. Once found, he would take full control.

Zuniga never offered to compromise unless at the bottom of the agreement the benefits were all his. It made him very suspicious of compliments.

"Capitan Zuniga, you are a fine military man," observed Don Dominguez over a glass of brandy. "You are new here, but you have kept order exceptionally well. Why, I imagine that it is only petty jealousy on the part of your superiors that keeps you from rising to the position you deserve."

Captain Zuniga put down his glass with an audible clink, as if his every action required military precision. He leaned over the mahogany table, his piercing eye above the saber scar on his cheek boring into the ranchero's. "Don Jose," he said in clipped words, "you did not bring me here to compliment me or discuss my career. What is the purpose of this meeting?"

"You are very direct. I like that also." Dominguez offered the crystal decanter to the captain, who shook his head. The ranchero refilled his own glass and sipped it before continuing.

"I intend to own a much larger rancho than I do at present when the mission lands are secularized," began the Don.

"So," said Zuniga abruptly, "what has this to do with me? Figueroa decides when—if ever—it will take place, and his appointee will be in charge of the distribution."

"Just so," agreed Don Jose, "exactly my point. Don't you see that timing is everything? We must be ready to present claims for the newly available land and help the governor make up his mind."

"Why do you say 'we'? I am neither a ranchero nor a confidant of Figueroa."

"But you are ambitious, are you not, my good capitan? You would rise in rank and prestige?"

"And salary," added Zuniga. "I wish to own a fine house and be wealthy. I will not retire with a 'thank you' and a few hectares of land on which to grub out an existence."

"Of course not." Don Jose eyed the thin lips of the smaller man and knew he had judged Zuniga's greed correctly. "Let me pose a question to you: What would Figueroa do if there was a revolt among the neophytes?"

"He would order me to crush it, as was done here in '24."

"And if he were convinced that the padres' mismanagement had caused the revolt, what then?"

Zuniga studied the question for a minute, then smiled. "He would be convinced that it was time to complete the secularization of the missions, but not transfer the property to the Indios."

"Again, just so. And what better person to advise him on the proper distribution of the lands than the military hero who crushed the revolt?"

Captain Zuniga sat back in the finely carved chair, contemplated his glass, and then raised it in salute. "You may count on me," he affirmed.

Don Jose lifted his own glass and touched it to the rim of the captain's. "Your very good health, capitan. I was certain we would see eye to eye on this matter."

CHAPTER 3

The old Indian did not expect to find the man alive. What the desert covered with a mantle of sandstorm, it most often claimed for its own. Still, there was always a chance that a member of his own tribe, stolen by the Mojaves, had escaped. It had happened before that a woman or a child managed to avoid recapture and find their way back to the valley.

For this reason Falcon had descended farther into the barren landscape than his herb gathering normally took him. His grandson, Blackbird, riding easily on his grandfather's back, scanned the stony face of the cliffs with his sharp, young eyes.

"See, Grandfather, sitting against that rock."

Falcon's eyes followed the line of his grandson's thin brown arm and pointing finger. A figure in scuffed and dirty buckskins was resting against the shady side of a boulder. The knees were drawn up and a head could be seen lolling back on the curved surface of the stone.

"Stay here, Blackbird," said Falcon, setting the boy down. He added sternly, "Don't follow me unless I tell you to come."

Falcon approached the reclining form cautiously. He studied the man from a dozen feet away. What he saw was a powerfully built man with dark red hair and beard. The man's eyes, though closed, appeared sunken into his head and the skin over his cheekbones was stretched tight.

It was several minutes before Falcon detected the faint flutter of breath in the man's chest. He unslung his doeskin water bottle from around his neck and untied the rawhide thong that closed its neck.

Cupping his palm beneath the man's mouth, Falcon carefully poured a small amount of the precious fluid into his hand. At first the unconscious man seemed insensible to the moisture presented to his lips. In another moment the lips began to work, sucking the drips from Falcon's palm.

Falcon added another small amount of water to his hand, and the man drank it greedily. Strong throat muscles worked as if his gullet were trying to reach out and grasp the source of the moisture.

Falcon poured another handful of water, watching the opening of the container carefully as he did so. When he looked back at the man's face, Falcon was startled to find the eyes open and staring into his.

He controlled himself with difficulty, fighting the instinct to jump back. "Ojos verdes," he murmured softly, giving the Spanish for *green eyes*. Falcon's own language had no reference to eye color, since none of his people had any other shade than brown.

Will looked into the clear brown eyes of Falcon and read there concern and some confusion, but no animosity.

Will gestured toward the water sack as a plea for another drink. Falcon presented it without hesitation, letting Will drink his fill.

"Thank you," gasped Will, when he had finished swallowing half the bag's contents. "Thank you," he repeated, nodding his head and handing the water sack back.

"Español?" asked Falcon with a questioning tone to his voice.

"No, not Spanish," answered Will. "American."

"A-mare-can. Smit. A-mare-can."

Will shook his head to indicate that his fuddled brain did not comprehend. When Falcon extended the drinking sack again, Will gladly accepted and took another long swallow.

Falcon tried again to communicate his understanding of the word American. "Smit," he intoned.

Something clicked in Will's memory then, something he had carried since the trappers' rendezvous when Jedidiah Smith had shared his tales of California.

"Smith? You mean Jedidiah Smith?"

Falcon nodded, smiling, his prominent nose bobbing up and down. "Smit, yes. Trap-per."

"A trapper. Yes, that's what I am," agreed Will, pointing to his chest.

Both men sat in silent appreciation of their first clear communication. Then the old Indian seemed to decide something. He turned his head and made a short, birdlike sound. A moment later a small, round-eyed boy wearing only a breech clout stood beside the old man. He gazed at Will with frank curiosity and Will appraised them both with the same interest.

The child appeared to be eight or nine years old. His shoulder length hair was parted in the middle, and a headband of woven reeds braided with blackbird feathers encircled his head. He wore two strings of tiny round sea shells around his neck. His frame was small and skin color much darker than that of the desert Indians from whom Will had fled.

Will's eyes lingered on the shell necklace. Smith had spoken of Indians beyond the great Sierra mountains who used shells as money. These two must be far from home if that was the case.

The old man was unsmiling. Also dark and of small stature, he, too, wore a choker of larger shells around his withered neck. Falcon-feather ear ornaments hung to his shoulders. His headband was made from the down of an eagle. He had a deep scar on his upper left arm. *Probably the wound of an arrow*, Will thought. A longer scar across his left ribs had been made by a knife. The Indian lifted his chin and put a hand proudly on the shoulder of the young one.

"Chock," he said, then he touched the blackbird feathers of the boy's headband.

Chock sounded like the call of a blackbird. There was no mistaking the fact that the Indian boy's name was *Blackbird*.

Will pointed skyward and then back to the child. "Blackbird," he said the word in his own tongue. Then, "Chock."

The mouth of the old man twitched slightly as if this immediate understanding on the part of the white trapper pleased him. It did not surprise him, however.

Now he touched the falcon feather at his ear, then his own chest. "Limik," he intoned.

So the old one was called Falcon, a name of honor. Will raised his hand in the air and brought it down with the swiftness of a falcon falling upon its prey. "Falcon," he said, and then he repeated the Indian word as well. "Limik."

Will was pleased that the language of these Indians would be easy to master. Words seemed to take on the sound of the objects they labeled. The cry of a falcon did, in fact, sound very close to the name, *Limik*.

Now it was Will's turn, "Will Reed." He reached out to lay his finger against the child's reed headband. "*Reed*," he repeated as little Blackbird ducked away from his touch.

Falcon grabbed the child by the arm and scowled at him. He pulled off the headband. "*Reed*," he repeated. "*Español, Tule.*"

Tule was indeed the Spanish word for Reed! So the old man understood some Spanish! "Si!" Will cried with relief. At least simple communication would not be a problem. Were they mission Indians far from the California padres? Will had only heard about such folk from the handful of trappers who had actually been there. These people with their shell necklaces and dark skin; were they from the ocean called Pacific?

Will was not alone in his relief. Both Blackbird and Falcon grinned as Will continued in Spanish, "Are you from California? Mission Indians?"

"No," Falcon put an arm protectively around Blackbird. "In Español we are known as Tulereños."

"People of the Reeds?"

"Si," Falcon nodded. "We are a free people. The reed people. Not mission Indians."

Will had heard from the staunch Methodist, Smith, of the proud tribes of California who refused the protection of the mission fathers. For over fifty years the Spanish missions had clung tenaciously to the coast line of the fabled western land, but seldom did anyone of white blood venture into the vast interior valley with its great waterways and thick reeds. Those Indians who ran from the Catholic missions fled to the tules. Fifty years of runaways had been enough time for the Spanish language to come in bits and pieces even to Indians like these, Will knew.

"What do you call yourselves? In your own language?"

Falcon's chest puffed out and he shook back his long graying hair. "We are *Yokuts.*"

"Yokuts," Will repeated the word once, and then again.

This again pleased Falcon. It was a sign of respect for this dusty white man to know there was a difference between the name the Spanish had given his people and the one they had always carried. It was a good thing, his expression seemed to say, that they had come in search of the one who ran from the dreaded Mojaves.

The headman of the Reed People gestured for Blackbird to produce a buckskin stuff-sack from around his neck. Reaching in he withdrew three pieces of jerked venison which the three companions gnawed on in thoughtful silence.

His strength returning, Will was able to get to his feet. He picked up the knife. The American saw both Yokuts glance at the weapon.

"Mojaves attacked my . . ." he groped for a word. "My group, my tribe."

Falcon let out a long hissing noise that his grandson mimicked an instant later. "Mojaves fight Yokuts too."

The three formed into a line and set off toward the west. At six feet three, Will towered over Falcon's five feet six. Blackbird tried to march as stoically as his grandfather, but kept sneaking sly glances over his shoulder at the red-haired giant now following behind.

Their path wound up through a rocky ravine. The

creosote brush, boulders and Joshua trees looked no different to Will than countless other dry washes he had explored without result. The ground was parched and dusty.

When they turned into a canyon almost hidden from the desert floor by a low range of hills, Will could see that they were following a dry creek bed. Its meandering course led them to ever-higher elevations, where an occasional Yucca palm bloomed on the rubble-strewn slopes. The composition of the hillside changed to more rock and less dust, its uniform brown color giving way to streaks of red and orange.

The Indians showed no signs of weariness, but Falcon's consideration of Will was such that they paused every mile to let him lean heavily on a walking stick.

Presently, they filed into a cliff-sided arroyo where the climbing was even steeper. This passage soon gave way to a narrow grassy valley, dotted with oak trees. At the head of the valley the group paused and Falcon offered its name, "Te-ha-cha-pi." Was this the place Jedediah Smith had told Will about as they shared the warmth of a campfire?

Clouds had piled up against the line of mountain peaks surrounding the little valley. As the three made another descent, again their path beside a trickling brook and the oak-tree-covered hillsides gave proof of how much moisture was trapped by the encircling summits.

Denser growths of oak trees appeared and Will began to spot larger numbers of animals. He saw a lumbering bear, momentarily glimpsed retreating over a ridge, and a herd of pronghorns flung up their heads in uniform alarm. A corkscrew motion of their tails and half-a-hundred white rumps disappeared into a side canyon. The land was thick with game and Will remembered the awe of Smith's voice when he had spoken of it.

The little procession stopped again on a rounded grassy knoll. Will made his way up from the end of the line to stand beside Falcon and Blackbird. He expected to see a winding descent to another brushy canyon.

Just as Will lifted his eyes to the west, a shaft of sunlight broke through the cloud cover. "Trawlawwin," gestured Falcon, swinging his arm in an arc that took in all the view from south to north. "In Español, San Joaquin."

Before Will lay the broadest expanse of green valley he had ever seen. From its southern terminus at the Tehachapis, Will looked west across to the distant range of coastal mountains. To the northwest as far as he could see was the unbroken sweep of a vast plain stretching onward until grayish-white clouds and rolling emerald vistas merged. *"The Promised Land,"* Jed Smith had called it. *"Or maybe a glimpse of what heaven looks like!"*

Beams of light performed a show for Will, dazzling his vision with scene upon scene of startling beauty. Here a patch of brilliant orange flowers painted a broad splash of color on a verdant hillside. The next ray of sun roved over fields of wild oats. Just-forming heads swayed with the rush of breeze like vibrant waves breaking against the rust-colored rocks. Beyond a chorus of nodding purple blossoms and past marching ranks of yellow blooms, the winding silver ribbon of a great river flashed a momentarily brilliant reflection. Following the river's course backward, red-helmeted flowers drew Will's eyes up to the mountains on his left hand. There the sunlight revealed that part of what he had taken for clouds was really a fringing mantle of snow lingering on the highest peaks.

"It's beautiful," he exclaimed. "A crazy quilt of color made by God Almighty." He quoted the phrase Smith spoke when he described this place. Indeed, there were no adequate words for it.

The Yokuts may not have understood all his words, but they had no trouble deciphering his feelings. In a tone of awe undiminished by years of repeating the experience, Falcon murmured, "We say tish-um-yu, ah, flower-blooming-time."

It was beautiful, yes. The kind of vision that made a man's heart ache, and yet . . . There were other things about this land that Will had heard. Tales of tragedy and brutality. When Jedediah had described it, he had pulled out his well-worn Bible and issued this warning to the men who sat enraptured by his tale of the land beyond the Sierras: *"Beyond what a man can imagine, the place is. I cried out to God that I had found Eden once again in that great valley."* And then his eyes had locked on Will, as though he saw something in Will's future. *"Remember son, this warning . . . Even Eden had the serpent. It was in a place of perfect beauty that man brought Death to us all. . . ."*

CHAPTER 4

"You are most welcome, señoras y señoritas." Billy Easton swept off his straw hat. Bending over his white pantaloons and bare feet, he made a "leg" that was worthy of a French courtier.

The ladies coming on board the schooner-rigged vessel *Paratus* twittered behind their fans. All about the deck were spread the trade goods with which the *Paratus* was loaded: silks and laces from China, otter pelts from the Russians of northern California, exotic spices from Pacific islands with unpronounceable names.

Across one quarter mile of placid water from the schooner lay the presidio of Santa Barbara. The white-washed adobe walls and red tile roofs stood out clearly against the dark green hillsides. Further inland, but just as prominently in view, was the mission. The settlement bustled with activity on this fine spring afternoon and it was clear that all was well in the Mexican province of California.

Like a conjuror opening his program, Easton produced a silk handkerchief from out of nowhere and presented it to Francesca Rivera y Cruz. "A gift, so that we may bargain as friends, sweet lady."

Easton's courtesy earned him a blushing smile from

Francesca, but a swat on the arm with a folded fan from her chaperon, Doña Eulalia.

"Aunt, you must apologize to Señor Easton," demanded Francesca, a slender young woman with darting black eyes and creamy pale skin. "He was only being polite."

"He should not be so forward," announced Doña Eulalia loudly, to the amusement of Easton's crew. "And you should not be so brash as to accept a gift from this, this . . ." Words failed the good aunt, but the word *pirate* came to everyone's mind, including Easton's.

It was an image he cultivated. Easton had long before discovered that while men bargained for hides and tallow with dour faces and closely watched ledgers, women preferred romance with their trade goods. From the gold ring in his ear lobe to the long hair pulled straight back from his face and gathered in another gold ring at the back of his neck, Easton looked the part of a privateer.

The truth was almost as fanciful. The son of a Yankee whaling skipper and his Hawaiian wahine wife, Easton had inherited his father's love of the sea and his mother's rich brown skin and easy smile. He had shipped with his father at the age of eight as a cabin boy and been first mate of a trading schooner at eighteen.

Now a muscular and solid five-foot-ten-inch man of thirty-five, Billy Easton sold his wares—whether "pirated" or bargained fair and square—up and down the coast of Spanish California, charming ladies of all ages.

He produced another silk handkerchief with a flourish. "A thousand pardons, most excellent Doña Eulalia. I meant no offense. Naturally I wished to offer a sample of my humble goods, poor and unworthy though they are, in comparison to such noble beauty as you yourself possess."

Now it was the aunt's turn to blush, which she tried to hide behind the ever-present fan. With a coyness not exactly suited to her age, she simpered, "You are quite forgiven, señor. I am most protective of my niece and sometimes speak abruptly."

"Understandable and commendable," replied Easton, the barest hint of a smile escaping below his drooping moustache. Extending his arm in its billowing silk sleeve, he offered, "Will you honor me by allowing me to escort you on a tour of my wares?"

Completely taken in by Easton's charm, Doña Eulalia quite graciously accepted the invitation.

CHAPTER 5

Will and the Yokuts made a cold camp that first night, high above the rim of Eden. The valley floor grew dusky purple in the twilight and fingers of smoke rose skyward, marking widely scattered Indian villages below. Falcon pointed to a distant plume. "Our village," he said.

The boy chirped, "They thought we would return tonight. They will think the West has taken us." At this remark, the old man whirled as if to strike the child. But Blackbird was far too fast, dodging and scrambling across the boulder out of reach. He had broken some taboo, Will guessed. The Mojave Indian raiders were east of the valley. And yet was there something in the West more terrifying to the People of the Reeds?

Will did not ask the meaning of this comment. He understood the ways of the Indian. Some things were only spoken of in hushed and reverent tones in the shadowy steam of the village sweat house. Two years of living among the Cherokee nation had taught Will not to ask questions but to simply live and wait. The answers inevitably came in their own time.

Tonight he did not question the wisdom of the fireless camp. They were still on the fringe of territory where the Mojave raiders might track them. It would be foolish to offer the enemy proof that they remained within reach of attack. And yet, it was the distant western mountains that the old man scanned now. He stood for a long time on the flat table of a boulder, which jutted out from the side of the mountain. Only when the last purple silhouettes were lost in darkness did he finally turn away.

Falcon tossed a rabbitskin cloak to Will and then gently took the remorseful boy under his arm. The three ate jerked meat in silence, and then Blackbird and Falcon curled up together beneath the old man's cloak to ward off the chill of the Sierra night.

———

Will's back was against the rough hide of the boulder that had been warmed through the night by his body heat. It now returned the warmth to him. The predawn air was sharp beyond the rabbitskin cloak. Will opened his eyes, surprised to see that the old Indian had resumed his post on the rugged granite table. He had left his cloak spread over the sleeping child, and now, dressed only in his breech clout, he searched the western horizon for sign of the talking smoke. He seemed undaunted by the chill, and yet his senses were so keen, it was as if he heard Will open his eyes. Turning away from the west, he strode quickly back the two dozen paces to where Blackbird slept.

Without a word, he yanked the warm cloak from the boy who sat up and then jumped to his feet in one movement. Will stood as well and rolled up his covering, tossing it to the old man.

"We have far to go," said Falcon. "We will eat as we journey."

The light of the sun touched the distant western

mountain peaks before it seeped into the valley floor. The two Indians moved down the rugged trail like deer. Quick and agile, the old one moved with the same untiring endurance as the boy. It was plain to Will that the slow pace of yesterday's hike had been in consideration of the white man they traveled with. Now, after a night of rest, it was expected that Will would keep pace. His long stride and sure step did not slow them down.

The swiftness with which they covered the ground did not conceal the details of the country Jedediah had told him about. Men had doubted the tales of wonder as they listened, but now Will knew his trapper friend had reported truthfully.

The rest of the trek to the Yokut encampment was one of vision upon vision and wonder upon wonder. Coveys of quail scurried at the walkers' approach, and no fewer than two hundred quail topknots bobbed into the gooseberry thickets with every flock they scattered.

Ground squirrel mounds extending for literal acres spoke of vast underground rodent cities. Overhead, redtailed hawks dived and soared.

"Swoop, swoop," pointed out Blackbird, indicating the redtails.

"Yes, they are swooping," responded Will.

"No, no. No swoo-ping. Swoop, swoop," insisted Blackbird.

Will gathered that what he had taken for an English expression describing the hawk's hunting motion was actually the Yokut name for the bird.

A muted bugling sound echoed up from the swampy area just ahead of their path. Two dozen thick-bodied elk moved from their grazing with an unhurried, deliberate motion. When the herd had put the marsh between themselves and the humans, they stood gazing back at the intruders.

It seemed impossible to Will that Jedediah's serpent could have found this Eden.

In the moist soil of the valley floor, the height of the grasses increased. Now the wild grain stalks waved over the flowers, hiding the brilliant colors from view. A vagrant wind parted the stalks, allowing a flash of crimson to come to Will's eyes, then concealing it again. A moment later and another stray breeze uncovered an expanse of orange, and so on, until it seemed that the swirling puffs of air were playing a guessing game with Will: What color would be revealed next?

It was late afternoon when they came to the banks of a swiftly flowing stream and turned to follow its course northeastward again toward the mountains. For the first time since descending the pass, they followed a recognizably human trail. And for the first time, Will felt that he and his two companions were not the first people to see this paradise.

The breeze carried the faint odor of smoke to Will's nostrils and with it he caught the welcome aroma of roasting meat. Blackbird now broke from his place in the middle of the march, running ahead to announce their return.

Before the village came into view, Will could hear Blackbird's excited chatter. The scout guessed that a proclamation of the white man's arrival was something the small boy wanted particular credit for.

Around one more bend of the river and they entered the encampment. A semicircle of reed huts surrounded a clearing with a cooking fire in its center. Two small children squealed and ran to hide behind a young woman who was working near the water's edge.

An older woman was tending the meat Will had smelled. Green willow poles were fixed in the ground around the cooking fire. To each stick was tied a rabbit carcass, and the weight of the meat pulled the stick down to the perfect roasting height above the fire.

In front of one of the huts, a ponderously heavy man was chipping arrow points on a buckskin ground cloth. He rose slowly to his feet, leaving his tools and obsidian rocks on the ground.

When the squealing children had been shushed, Will could tell that he was being introduced. He heard Falcon repeat his name and the designation "A-mare-can." The rest of the speech was not understandable, but must have related the circumstances of his rescue.

But the introduction was short-lived. A sharp shout from across the stream drew everyone's attention. A Yokut man, a hunter about Will's age, came out of the screen of willows directly opposite the camp and forded the creek.

He called Falcon's name. The warrior sounded excited about something, waving his arms and pointing back the way he had come.

Falcon left Will's side to join the newcomer. The heavy man who left his toolmaking entered the discussion also. Falcon's voice was quiet and questioning, the other two loud and angry.

Will wondered if the Mojaves had raided the valley ahead of his arrival. Maybe that was what this unsettling report was about.

The women and children were silent and staring. No one paid any attention to Will at all. He stood awkwardly at the edge of the encampment, waiting for the noisy tirade to subside.

The toolmaker seemed to remember Will first. He stretched out a thick, muscled arm and leveled a calloused finger at Will's face. The tone of his words was accusing and he was obviously blaming Will for whatever evil had just happened.

The toolmaker repeated the gesture, then accompanied it with a demanding slam of his fist into his hardened palm. Falcon's reply was a sudden emphatic cutting motion of his hand. In any language it meant "Enough!"

Falcon pivoted sharply on his heel and returned to the American. It seemed that now the entire camp was drawn up in a line confronting Will.

The old Indian explained, "Two hunters left our camp on the same day that I went east. They have not returned. That man, Coyote, says he followed their trail to the River of Swift Water, but no farther. He returned to bring word."

"Meho, the toolmaker, thinks you are the cause," Falcon added, "but he feels hate deep in his heart since his wife was taken by the West."

"I will help track the missing men," offered Will. He shook off Falcon's refusal. "I owe your people a debt and Meho must be shown how I will repay."

An hour later, Will was back at his profession—tracking. Falcon accompanied him, and the other two men went also, but they were not happy about Will's presence. The toolmaker, Meho, was openly angry, scowling at the scout whenever their eyes met. The other man was stoic but clearly suspicious. Each time Will looked in Coyote's direction, he found the warrior already watching him.

The tracks of the two missing hunters were not obvious, but clear enough to those who knew what to look for. A moccasined footprint showed occasionally in the dust. One of the two men was considerably larger than the other, as Will could tell from the greater length of his stride. The shorter man walked with a limp. His right foot made an indistinct track, as if he could not press the heel all the way down.

The trail ended abruptly at the bank of a river that was indeed swift flowing. Grass growing along the edges of the watercourse was stretched out flat against the bank by its force. When Will spotted a twig in the current, he got only a brief glimpse before it completely disappeared.

The two warriors tied their bows and foxskin pouches of arrow points into compact bundles, which they slung over their backs. Both men plunged into the water, pushing hard for the opposite shore. Falcon turned to the scout. "Do you swim, Will Reed?"

When Will responded that he did, the old man replied, "Good. Then we will not need to carry you."

The water was bitterly cold, and the current so powerful, that Will could make no headway against it. He wasted no time fighting it, but took a long angle toward a bend of the river downstream and let the water carry him there.

Will was the last to cross. The others had already restrung their bows and were prepared to continue the search. The big man, Meho, sneered at Will and said something contemptuous to Coyote.

A brief search of the shore located the spot where the two hunters had emerged from the river. Several tracks in the mud of the bank were evident. Will spotted a flint arrowpoint under a bush where it must have fallen from the hunter's pouch.

The three Yokuts became noticeably tense. The river seemed to mark a boundary between known and unknown, between safety and danger. There was no obvious sign of a greater hazard nor any indication that enemies had been near the two missing men. Still, Will scanned the rolling hills that marched along beside them. He kept a close eye on the treetops ahead for any unusual flights of birds that might betray the presence of others.

The trail was proving harder to follow now. It was obvious the two men had been hunting. They had separated and were travelling about one hundred yards apart. Will and Falcon were following the one with the limp. In about a mile, the tracks showed that the man had turned aside to stand on a rocky outcropping and survey the landscape.

When he did the same, Will noted a swampy area of thick grass just beyond a screen of elderberry bushes. It was a perfect spot for game, with plenty of cover to approach from behind. Will and Falcon headed that direction.

Will studied the area around the berry bushes till he found what he was seeking. A half moccasin print next to a shallow round depression in the soil showed where the hunter had knelt to take aim.

Looking across the clearing from this vantage point, the scout picked out a likely spot under an oak where he could imagine a deer to have stood. A dark stain on the ground just under the oak confirmed the accuracy of Will's guess. The trail of occasional drops of blood mingled with the curious halting steps of the limping man, and both led to the west.

When the two trackers heard a rustling coming toward them through the brush, they froze in place under the shadow of the oak. Falcon's gnarled hands fitted an arrow with a jagged obsidian point to his bow. He dropped to one knee and drew the bowstring back to his ear.

A moment later the Yokut chief and the white trapper both relaxed. The sound had only been Meho and Coyote. The man with the limp had apparently called his companion to rejoin him in following the wounded deer.

Together the four followed the track that was again plain to read. A vagrant swirl of air reached them. Death was on the breeze; the sick-sweet, metallic odor of decay. The three Indians instinctively fanned out across the trail, their bows at the ready. Will drew his Green River knife and moved from tree to tree, crossing open spaces with a rush, then stopping to look around. Overhead, a flight of vultures spiralled.

Ahead was an oak, seventy feet tall, with a large limb that jutted out a dozen feet off the ground. From this limb hung the bloated carcass of a deer, the deadly shaft of the arrow plainly visible just behind its shoulder.

And underneath the deer was the body of a man. Scavengers had already been at work on the flesh, but the twisted right leg told Will that this had been the man with the limp.

Falcon knelt beside the body, taking a handful of dust from the ground and sprinkling some on the corpse. The rest he poured on his own head. In silent mourning he lifted up his arms toward the sun, let them fall, then lifted them again.

Meho and Coyote stood as sentinels to this grief. They watched the surrounding area, scanning both near and far.

Will continued to search. Not far from the tree, a struggle had taken place, with torn up earth and uprooted plants testifying to its fierceness. Then at last a flattened space, where the uncoiling spirals of orange fiddleneck had been crushed by a man-shaped press. Two long streaks mutely bore witness that the other missing Yokut had been dragged away.

Will followed the drag mark to the edge of a tule swamp, where some horses had been tethered. One of the horses had shied violently, perhaps as an unfamiliar burden was loaded onto its back. The riders had then departed, heading west, skirting the outline of the swamp. There was nothing further to be learned here, Will thought. Or was there? He stopped and puzzled over something. One rider had been mounted on a mare. The position of the hoofprints where the animal had relieved itself made this clear.

But a mare was an unusual choice for a mount. Most riders believed stallions and mares were too much trouble and often unpredictable as saddle animals. Geldings were the usual selection. *Of course*, Will thought, *that logic only applies to riders who have a choice.* Indians thereabouts would have to make do with whatever runaway stock they could catch.

Returning to the place of death, Will found that the body of the dead Yokut had been wrapped in Falcon's rabbitskin cloak. The three Indians were preparing to return to their village.

"Wait," the scout said to Falcon. "The other man is alive. Or at least he was when he was taken. I found where whoever did this mounted up. We can still follow."

"Which way do the tracks lead?" asked Falcon mournfully.

"To the west," reported Will, "and just as plain as day. If we were to—"

Falcon shook his head, but before Will could say any more, Meho jumped between them. He waved his arms and shouted angrily again, then he pushed Will in the chest, hard.

"What is it? What's he saying now?" Will demanded of Falcon, who was trying to grasp Meho's arm. Meho roughly shrugged off the chief's grip and moved toward Will.

"He says it is a trap. He says you are here to lead us right into their clutches. I tell him to stop, not shame us, he . . ."

Meho was in a blood rage, and like his namesake, the bear, he could not be called off easily. He drew a wicked-looking, curved-blade knife from a deerhide sheath that hung by his side and lunged at Will.

The trapper barely had time to throw himself to the side. The slashing knife missed, but Meho's massive shoulder crashed into Will, knocking him to the ground.

Will rolled completely over and bounced to his feet. His red beard brushed up fragments of wildflowers as he rolled.

The toolmaker rushed in again. This time Will stood his ground and let the anger-blinded man come. The American caught the upraised knife-arm in both hands, and the two stood momentarily locked almost face to face. Will wondered if he had made a mistake, because Meho was immensely strong in his forearms and hands. But before the stout Yokut could force the blade down toward Will, the taller white man used his Mississippi upbringing to good effect.

Will backheeled the Indian, setting him up by yanking the knife hand unexpectedly down, then pushing up suddenly. The off-balanced Meho toppled to the sweep of Will's leg. He fell with the American on top of him and the blade of his own knife pressed across his throat.

"Tell him," gasped Will, "tell him I could kill him now if I wanted to." After Falcon had translated these words, Will continued, "And tell him I am not leading anyone into a trap."

"He understands," agreed Falcon. "You may let him up now, Will Reed. He will fight you no more."

The two men stood up, brushing off the dirt and leaves. Will hesitated, then reversed the knife and extended it handle first toward Meho.

"Now," Will said to Falcon, "let's get after the raiders."

The Yokut chief still shook his head no. "The West has taken him, Will Reed. If we follow, neither our tribe nor yours would ever see us again. Let us go back to camp." He gestured toward the cloaked body lying on the ground. "I have a son to bury."

CHAPTER 6

A steady stream of Indian women flowed uphill toward the mission. Each carried a single heavy adobe-brick building block. A second file returned, but these women were not empty-handed. The downhill stream carried bundles of straw to the mixing pits.

In groups of three, Indian men milled around in mud up to their knees, stamping straw, clay and water together to form the substance known as adobe. Another circuit of laborers piled the mixture into rawhide aprons, which they carried to the waiting wooden forms. There another set of men were smoothing off the blocks, turning bricks over to complete the drying process and stacking completed bricks.

There was no grumbling amongst the workers, but there was no enthusiasm either. For every team of nine workers, the object was to complete seven hundred bricks just as quickly as possible.

"You have gotten these miserios well organized," observed Don Dominguez to Captain Zuniga, "but I still object to your quota system. Letting these wretches quit when they have filled their allotment only makes my workers want to do likewise. I have heard that some groups finish work at midday and are allowed to do nothing all afternoon."

"It is not *my* quota system, as you well know," retorted the officer. "It has been the rule of the mission since these disgraciados were first coaxed into covering their naked bodies. Besides, I have already raised the quota twice, over the objections of Father Sanchez."

Dominguez snorted with derision at the name of the kindly priest. The noise he made startled the palomino horse on which he sat, and his gelding bumped into Zuniga's bay.

The bay reared slightly, and Don Jose's horse sidled away from it, stepping down into one of the adobe mixing pits. Dominguez shouted and swore, turning the confused horse around and around until one of the Indian workers grasped the cheekpiece of the bit and led the horse to firmer footing. The Indian muttered under his breath, "Gauchapin."

Dominguez overheard the phrase and slashed downward with his quirt, striking the man who had just come to his aid on the shoulder. The man actually drew his arms back as if he were about to leap onto the ranchero, but two of his comrades intervened and pulled him away.

"Did you see that impertinent scoundrel?" demanded Dominguez. "He was going to strike me! Zuniga, I want that man hanged! Gauchapin! Spur, he called me! Hang him, do you hear?"

The spectacle of the overweight ranchero having a tantrum while his agitated horse kicked up spatters of mud on the military commander brought all work to a sudden halt.

"Back to work, all of you!" shouted Zuniga. "Julio," he said to the native foreman, "bring that man to my office when you finish work today. That's an order." To the ranchero he observed, "Come, Don Dominguez. I will discipline that rebel personally."

The two rode on toward the shore. Dominguez turned around every few steps to curse and shake his fist at the Indians. Zuniga picked globs of mud from his uniform.

"What's the matter with you?" asked the ranchero petulantly. "We, gente de razón, were insulted! Why didn't you kill him right where he stood?"

"Calm yourself," the captain suggested in a quietly authoritative tone. "Should I kill a valuable worker? *You* of all people should know the *value* of every miscreant soul."

When Dominguez turned at the abrupt change in the quality of the officer's voice, Zuniga continued. "There is an important matter which we are going to discuss."

He gestured out toward where the *Paratus* was anchored in the bay. The ship's tender was coming ashore with some returning customers. "When I was last on board Easton's ship to review his cargo, he asked me about a certain cove a few miles north of here. He wanted to know if I had heard any rumors about any midnight loading of . . ." The rest of the sentence was allowed to flutter away on the sea breeze.

Dominguez froze, sitting very erect in his saddle. "I don't know what you are talking about," he muttered.

"Don't toy with me," threatened the officer coldly. "What you are doing is illegal. We both know that I could have you arrested and sent away in chains."

"But you wouldn't do that. We are partners," whined the ranchero.

"Partners must never have secrets from each other," said Zuniga flatly. "Never again. You should have told me, Don Dominguez. Now your avarice is going to cost you." Cold, black eyes turned fully on the rancher's face like a white shark out in the channel that had selected a seal to devour.

"Agreed! Agreed!" said Dominguez too eagerly. "I was going to tell you everything. Really. You must come to my hacienda and we can review the details. But what about Easton? How much does he know?" The ranchero was anxious to change the subject.

"Easton is not a problem. I am the only law that matters here, remember? I will take care of him if it becomes necessary," concluded the captain. Don Dominguez felt a shiver run down his neck as he heard these words.

The small boat from the *Paratus* was coming through the surf. Two sailors were rowing strongly, while the mate of the *Paratus* managed the tiller to keep the boat square to the waves. Timing the run perfectly, the boat shot forward on the mate's command and beached itself on the white sand.

The two caballeros watched as a group of women were assisted from the boat. Several bundles of their purchases were passed to them. The ladies waved cheerfully to the sailors who turned the tender around and floated it out to shove off. One of the women, Dominguez noted, was the beautiful daughter of Don Pedro Rivera y Cruz.

He turned to point her out to Zuniga, but found the officer already staring at Francesca. He continued staring as the group of women came up the beach and passed near them, the eyes of the shark still evident.

"Good day to you, ladies," called out Dominguez cheerfully. A polite murmur of greetings replied, except from Francesca, who walked with her eyes on the sand.

She had seen his companion's hungry stare.

When they had passed, Dominguez remarked to Zuniga, "I do not think she cares for the way you look at her."

"All women desire a man's mastery," said Zuniga with a shrug. "Some conquests take longer than others, that is all. She will be mine."

"It would not be well to let her father hear you say that," observed the ranchero. "He would horsewhip you. Besides," continued Don Dominguez, "I now know how to cement our partnership."

CHAPTER 7

The crackle of the flames rising above the tule-thatched hut was deafening. A thick trunk of dense gray smoke sprouted from the fire like a seed germinating into a tree of pointless destruction.

No one made any attempt to quench the inferno. To prevent the fire from spreading, those Yokuts who lived on either side of the dead man's dwelling had taken the precaution of wetting down their homes, but that was all.

Will had seen this practice before. Other tribes also burned the homes of their dead. There was a finality, an absoluteness, to the end of Indian life that Will found unsettling.

As soon as the pyre was ignited and the first tendrils of smoke twisted skyward, the other Yokuts turned away. In fact, they did everything to make life appear as normal as possible. An ancient crone directed the grinding and leaching of acorn meal. Two hunters prepared to leave the camp in search of game. Only Will and Blackbird stood silently watching the hut being consumed.

In contrast to the morning's studied nonchalance, the dance for the dead had lasted the entire preceding night. For hours on end the women of the tribe jumped and swayed around a campfire, while the men chanted a funeral dirge over and over. The night was punctuated by the beating of log drums until all the listeners felt their breath and heartbeat become one with the rhythm. After hours of the monotonous pounding, Will noticed that even a temporary silence caused him to be filled with a sense of anxiety and foreboding.

Gifts of food, clothing, baskets and tools were all brought to the funeral ceremony, but not for the comfort for the bereaved family. Instead, as each dancer reached exhaustion, the gifts were tossed onto the blazing fire.

But now, the morning after, the savage excitement of the ceremony had worn off and was replaced by a blank numbness compounded by weariness. Blackbird stared into the dancing flames as the charred ribs of the willow framework crumpled into what had been the interior of his home.

Will walked up to the silent boy and put his hands on the thin shoulders. Blackbird's hands flew up to his face and small clenched fists ground into his eyesockets.

"I am not crying," insisted the child, though Will had asked no question. "It is the smoke that makes the water come from my eyes."

The scout said nothing, just stood quietly with his resting hands offering the comfort of a touch. Will was remembering himself as a young, red-haired boy with freckles, about Blackbird's age. A grieving child standing beside two mounds of earth back in the red clay hills of Tennessee.

The trapper shook his head, as if to make the image go away, but the hollow, empty ache remained. Will knew that the boy would be well cared for by his grandfather, but that would not lessen the anguish of missing both his murdered father and the mother who had died before.

Here was Eden, truly, but it was an Eden after Adam's fall. All the freedom to live, to hunt, to fish, to swim came to lie in the ashes of the now-smoldering hut. Evil walked in this land, and it brought death.

What was worse, Will knew that these people had no clear picture of a life beyond this patch of earth. Many Indians spoke in vague terms of a Happy Western Land, but they did not know where it was or how to reach it. Sometimes their stories told that the beyond was a great forest in which a soul might wander forever without rest.

The Yokuts danced and chanted themselves to numbness. They tried as quickly as possible to put the reminders of a missing loved one behind them. It was their way of avoiding the awful question, "After this life, what?"

"Father," the boy suddenly cried. "Do not get off the path!"

Several adult Yokuts cast disapproving looks at Blackbird's show of grief. And elderly woman said, "Shh! Enough!"

"Do not get off the path," the boy repeated, unheeding. "It may be dark there. There may be thorn bushes and steep cliffs. If you fall from the path, how will you find it again?"

Will sat beside Blackbird and slipped an arm around the boy's shoulders. "I am not old enough," the boy exclaimed, "to know how to track well. How can I learn to walk where the trail is dim and unknown?"

The red-bearded scout spoke in a quiet voice, yet his words echoed with strength in Blackbird's hollow-feeling heart. "I know the path," he said, "—that is, I know the One who *is* the path."

"What do you mean?" asked the boy.

"Blackbird, all men everywhere are fearful about what lies beyond this life. We would *have* to be afraid of it, except for this fact: God, the one you call the Great Spirit, sent his son Jesus to scout the trail for us. You see, he not only took a punishment of death in place of us, but he came to life again, and he says he will show us how to walk beyond this life."

"Tell me some more about this man! He must be the greatest tracker who ever lived."

"And much more," the scout replied. "He will blaze a trail for you in this life also, if you will let him."

Will turned Blackbird to face him. "Listen. I need your help as well," he said.

The Indian boy rubbed his eyes again, then peeped out past one. "What do you mean?"

"I am going to stay with your people for a time," answered Will. "But I am ignorant of your ways. I need someone to teach me, to show me how a proper Yokut acts."

The boy straightened up and squared his shoulders. "I am the grandson of a chief. My fa . . ." his voice faltered. "*I* will be chief someday. I will teach you so you need not be ashamed."

———

The stillness of a soft, spring afternoon was interrupted by a messenger from another camp upstream. The man, Badger by name, brought news that a party of Mojaves had come over the pass from the desert. Badger had been surrounded while hunting, but had been allowed to go free in order to bring word that the Mojaves wanted a parley.

"What does it mean?" asked Will.

"Who can say?" shrugged Falcon. "The Mojaves raid the valley, robbing and killing. If they want to talk, they must want something that they cannot easily get by stealing."

The smoldering cooking fire was refueled. When it was blazing, a bundle of water-soaked reeds was placed on top to send up a thick column of white smoke that signaled the Mojaves to come down into the camp.

No more sound than the barest rustle of wind among dry leaves preceded the arrival of the desert people. Six warriors and a leader glided into Falcon's village under the watchful eyes of a dozen Yokut men. The women and children were out of sight, hiding in the tule huts.

Will stood inside the doorway of the hut he shared with Falcon and Blackbird. No one had asked him to help guard the camp, but no one had told him to stay away either. He felt a stirring at the back of his neck when the Mojaves came into view.

The desert tribesmen were taller than most of the Yokut men Will had seen. Their complexions were several shades lighter than the valley people, as if designed to blend easily into the sands of their home. They wore their hair long, down even below their shoulders. Unlike the Yokuts, who went barefoot or wore buckskin moccasins, the Mojaves wore sandals made of woven Yucca fibers.

The faces of the desert warriors were etched with ferocity and deep scowls. For men who supposedly had come to talk, Will noted that they had not come empty-handed. Each had a short bow made of willow branches, and at his side was a short wooden club, shaped like a sickle with a round handle on one end and a flattened killing point on the other.

The leader of the Mojaves wasted no time on ceremony. He addressed Falcon in words unknown to Will, but conveying a tone of angry demands. His speech was accompanied by vigorous gestures to the south and the west, then with an exaggerated show of surprise toward the east.

The Mojave held up all ten of his fingers and displayed them to Falcon three times. Then, as if to prove a point, he reached into a rabbitskin pouch hanging around his neck and withdrew a knife. He flipped the weapon so that it stuck quivering in the ground between them.

Will could not help starting forward in horror—the knife standing upright in the soil of the Yokut village was a twin to the one Will had taken from Forchet.

As Will moved from the shadowed doorway of the hut, the Mojave leader took notice of the white man for the first time. The desert warrior first stared at him, then bent quickly and retrieved the knife from the ground.

Will pulled the other blade from his belt and advanced with coldly set anger toward the Mojave. The other desert Indians had nocked arrows to bowstrings, an action mirrored by the Yokut warriors. One wrong move and a fully pitched battle would break out.

Falcon shouted a command for Will to stop where he was. Without turning his back on the Mojave, Falcon continued calling out instructions.

"You will not come one step closer," Falcon ordered the angry scout. "You must put up your knife at once. You are not permitted to disturb the parley in this way."

"Ask him where he got the Green River knife," Will replied.

"He has already said he took it from a Mexican chief whose men attacked their village. He came here to propose that we join them in fighting against the Mexicans."

Will answered quietly, but his muscles were as tense as a coiled spring. "The truth is, he took that from Beckwith, another American and a friend of mine, after the Mojaves ambushed us without any reason!"

The two chiefs spoke together again. Turning toward Will, Falcon said, "Sihuarro says you were spying for the Mexicans and that thirty of you were killed attacking his people."

With icy calm Will responded, "There were only twelve of us and we never saw them till they jumped us. We traded peacefully with every tribe we met on the trail till these scorpions attacked. Tell him I said that."

"Do you know what may happen if I return your words to Sihuarro? If he chooses, he may fight you here and now to prove you have insulted him."

"Let her rip," replied Will calmly.

Falcon spoke to the Yokut guards, telling them to carefully let the tension off their bowstrings while the Mojaves did the same. Then, the Yokut headman said one word to Sihuarro, very quietly but very distinctly. It was the Mojave word for *liar*.

What followed was a smear of movement across what had been a painted scene. Sihuarro shifted the knife to his left hand and raised his killing stick with his right.

There was a whirring sound like an angry bee. Catching a glimpse of a blurred threat spinning toward his head, Will lifted his left arm to shield his face and nearly was too late: The killing stick smashed into his forearm, cutting a long shallow arc of a wound, then nicked his ear as it completed its murderous path.

Will pressed his injured arm against his chest and prayed that its instantly total numbness would quickly go away. From the corners of his vision he saw that the two opposing lines of warriors had closed into a circle around the fight. Then all his attention was focused on Sihuarro who rushed toward him brandishing the knife overhead. The Mojave intended to end the fight quickly with a killing stroke.

But the speed of the attack was his undoing. With a presence of mind born more of instinct than conscious thought, Will waited until Sihuarro was almost on him, then ducked under the descending blade. The trapper put his shoulder into the Indian's midsection and turned the attacker's momentum to his advantage.

With the same stretch and leverage used to hoist a hundred-weight of beaver pelts, Will propelled Sihuarro up and over his back. The Indian landed with a jarring thud, but rolled into a ball and jumped up again to face Will.

Circling each other warily, the opponents looked for an opportunity to strike. Blood from the cut on Will's arm dripped from his elbow onto the dark earth. Neither fighter looked up when a condor soaring overhead momentarily shadowed the scene. Again it was Sihuarro who could not wait, springing toward Will. This time the moment was more controlled, and the Indian's Green River knife was held low, blade upward. The blow was aimed toward Will's belly with a stab and a slash up.

But Will met the move blade to blade. Using the skinning knife like a short sword, he parried the thrust in a clang of steel. What he could not parry was a rake of the Mojave's left hand that tore across his eyes.

With a cry of pain, Will threw himself to the side away from the Indian's knife hand. One of his eyes began to stream tears and immediately began to swell shut. Sihuarro closed again, the knife straight forward.

This time there was no opportunity to meet the thrust and only an instant to duck out of the way. Will spun around and locked his hands on Sihuarro's wrist, but the injury to the trapper's left arm had left it still partly numbed and weak. Will used the butt of the knife handle to hammer on Sihuarro's hands.

Before he could make the Mojave drop the knife, a snake-like arm groped over Will's head. Long fingernails began probing for Will's eyes, making him squirm and duck.

The trapper smashed his skull into the Indian's face. The Mojave lost interest in raking the white man's eyes, reaching too late to cover his own shattered nose.

Putting his rough-and-tumble upbringing among river toughs to good use, Will snapped the chief's knife-arm upward, then yanked it down. With a mighty heave, he swung the warrior over his hip and to the ground.

"Two falls to none," he growled.

The savage had underestimated the white man's strength and fighting ability. Sihuarro sprang up before Will could press his advantage, but not so quickly as before.

Both men eyed each other, catching their breath. "I will enjoy giving your head to my dogs for their sport," hissed Sihuarro in English.

"I thought so," muttered Will. Then louder, "You'd best rethink that plan. I grew up wrestlin' Tennesseans, and the littlest one not so scrawny as you."

The Mojave moved toward Will's left, pressuring the

trapper's injured arm and blinded eye. Another sudden lunge and a slash forced Will to circle quickly to his right.

Sihuarro repeated the move, trying to take advantage of Will's weaker quarter. A third time he made the same play, and Will stumbled, feigning a slip.

This time the chief came in farther and faster. At the last instant, Will ducked the opposite direction to the feint, leaping to his left. He slashed down hard with his own blade on the warrior's forearm.

Sihuarro gave a cry of pain, then spun away from Will, yanking his damaged knife-arm back toward his body.

The trapper jumped toward him. Sihuarro made a wild, backhand slash that Will only avoided by throwing himself flat. He lashed out with his right foot as he fell, kicking hard against the Indian's knees.

The Mojave chief tried to leap over the leg sweep, but Will's back foot caught and he heaved upward with all his strength. Sihuarro fell heavily on his side, plunging his own weapon into his side between the fifth and sixth ribs. He yanked the blade out of the wound with a shriek, then rolled face-down and was still.

The fight was over. Will dragged himself wearily to his feet. He felt no particular sense of victory, just gratitude at being alive. Sihuarro lay still in the dust of the Yokut camp. The spreading crimson pool widening beneath his motionless body gave mute testimony to the severity of his wound.

Will scanned the faces of the Indian onlookers. The Mojaves reflected sullen hatred, the Yokuts a stoic indifference. Falcon stepped forward from behind Will and stood silently at the trapper's elbow.

The Yokut chief offered Will the Green River knife that had fallen from Sihuarro's fingers. "Take it," he urged, "it is yours now."

Will accepted the knife, but still no one in the circle moved. "What's happening?" he asked Falcon. "What are they waiting for?"

"Are you not going to cut off his head?" inquired Falcon earnestly. "The others of the desert are waiting to take his body back with them."

"Your people do this?" asked Will.

"It is our custom," returned the chief in a matter-of-fact tone. "Otherwise the warrior's spirit may return to the body and seek revenge."

"Well, it's not my custom," answered Will flatly. "Tell them to take him and go. He might still be alive. Don't they care?"

Falcon shook his head. "Even if he lives, he is a defeated warrior. He will have to fight many times among his own people to lead them again." He kicked dirt on Sihuarro's body and jerked his head toward the Mojaves as if to say, "Take this lump of earth out of here."

"Wake up, my friend," urged Falcon. "Come to the sweat house with me. When we are purified and bathed, your wound will heal faster and not feel so stiff."

Downstream from the camp was a willow and tule hut similar to the Yokut sleeping lodges, except that this hut was partly sunken in the ground and the exterior was covered with a plaster of mud. The inside temperature was already above a hundred degrees from an oak fire.

In no time Will's body cast off the morning chill and

soon he began to perspire. Will wondered at the timing of this invitation—it was the first since he had come to the Yokut village. The events of the previous day seemed to have gained him a new acceptance with these people. He picked at the moss poultice bound around his wounded arm.

"Falcon," Will wondered out loud, "have I brought trouble on your people with the killing yesterday? Will the Yokuts be blamed?"

"Put your mind at rest," answered the Indian. "There is no love between the Yokuts and the Mojaves. We would have listened to their speech, then sent them home. We do not trust them and we do not want their quarrel with the Mexicans."

"Then I may stay here longer?" asked Will.

"Of course," Falcon replied. "As long as you wish. But first," he commanded, "come into the stream and wash off the white man stink!"

The two men tumbled out the opening into the cool morning air. It was well that the sweat house stood just above the creek because it gave Will no time to consider the next action. As it was, he tumbled down the bank after Falcon without stopping and plunged waist deep into icy water.

"Phew!" Will sputtered to his Indian brother. "You do this for fun?"

"Every day," returned Falcon. "We spend half our lives in the water. It is our friend."

"Maybe so," replied Will, "but it sure doesn't like me yet!"

———

In the days following the fight, Will discovered that

his relations with the Yokuts had changed in a subtle way. No longer their guest, now he was an accepted member of the clan. The early morning plunge into the stream never became a pleasure for the scout, but he adopted it as a part of the Yokut daily routine.

Another kind of adoption took place as well. Will went looking for Blackbird and found the boy sitting beside the remains of his father's hut. The child was idly picking up handfuls of ash and sifting them through his fingers, letting the east wind blow them away.

Will sat down cross-legged next to Blackbird. For a time neither spoke. Blackbird stared into the west as if watching the minute particles of dust float beyond the sight of mortal eyes.

"Blackbird," Will called softly, "I seem to recall your promise to teach me some things. It is time that I had a hut of my own. Will you show me the proper way to build it?"

The boy was short on enthusiasm, but he was agreeable. He and the scout tramped downstream toward the marsh to select reeds for the thatch.

Will stopped beside the bank of the creek to point out a clear footprint in the sand. "What is that?" he tested.

"Raccoon," replied the boy carelessly.

"And what was he doing here?"

The Yokut youth inspected the bank, noting the way the grassy turf overhung the water and was cut back underneath. "He was fishing for crayfish," replied the boy. Blackbird frowned in concentration, but Will could tell that the game was becoming enjoyable.

"Did he have a successful hunt?"

Blackbird was already scanning the banks as if he had anticipated this question. His gaze stopped, at last, a dozen feet downstream where a fallen tree stretched across an arm of the creek. The Indian boy scooted over to the branch and peered intently into the water.

"Ah," he said in triumph. "Raccoon sat here and ate his catch. Crayfish scales show where he picked apart and washed his food."

"Bravo!" applauded Will. "What a tracker you are."

The Yokut visibly brightened at this praise. He set to inspecting every inch of the trail for other signs that he could call to his friend's attention. "Deer. Coyote. Another deer. Skunk." Blackbird called the roll of every animal footprint he recognized. He looked at Will expectantly after each identification and smiled when Will gave him a nod of approval.

Up ahead, a thick patch of gray-green horehound surrounded the base of an oak, like a leafy collar around a neck of tree bark. Two does burst from this cover, sneaking off westward. They had jumped from their hiding even though the man and boy were still quite far and could not have seen them yet.

"Look!" exclaimed the excited boy. "Let's follow!"

"Hold on a minute," the scout warned. "Duck down behind this elderberry and watch . . ." Will inspected the surroundings, deciding at last on a buckeye tangle on a little knoll. "Watch the gully back of that knob."

A minute passed. Blackbird almost spoke, impatient with this unexplained lesson. With a shake of his head, Will cautioned him to remain silent. Once again the scout pointed toward the dry wash. A moment later, an old buck deer, hunched so low that he seemed to be walking on his knees, came sneaking out of his buckeye hiding place.

"That old buck sent those does out to distract us,

while he sneaks out the back door," explained Will.

The shine of hero worship was radiant in Blackbird's eyes as the two gathered the reed bundles for the scout's hut. Together they cut willow poles and formed these into a travois to drag the tule bundles to camp. The boy assured the scout that this was proper Yokut fashion: the willow poles would be lashed together to form the framework of the hut.

They spent the next day building the dome-shaped dwelling. It stood in line with the rest of the Yokut homes, but at the opposite end of the camp from the ashes of the boy's former home.

That night as Will and Blackbird shared a small fire in front of their finished construction, Falcon greeted them and sat.

"You have done well," he said to Will in approval.

"I had a good teacher," the scout acknowledged.

Falcon nodded solemnly. "Blackbird," he addressed his grandson, "I see that you are taking your duty to our new brother seriously."

The boy did his best to return an appropriately adult nod of agreement.

"Therefore," Falcon continued, "I direct that you stay in Will Reed's lodge and continue to teach him the Yokut ways. To Will he added, "And we must give you a name. You say you met the great Cherokee Chief Sequoyah, who stood as tall among his people as the red-barked tree stands in the forest. You are tall and red-haired, so we will call you Sequoyah."

CHAPTER 8

The Indian named Donato slumped on the cord binding his wrists. He was suspended at tiptoe level from an iron hook that protruded from a wooden beam.

"You are shamming, Donato," observed Father Quintana, "and it will do you no good. Let him have five more."

"But, Father," argued the Indian overseer wielding the whip, "he has received twenty-five lashes already." He pointed to Donato's bare back, already criss-crossed with cuts from the thin leather strap. Blood oozed from the mass of raw flesh and had spattered the wall by the hail of blows.

"Do not question me, Lazario, or you will hang there next," corrected the priest. "This one has carried the punishment pole, sat in the stocks, and still he persists in sneaking out at night. No more will I listen when he pleads he will reform. This will be a lesson he will remember forever!"

Lazario had raised his arm in preparation for another whistling stroke of the whip when the chamber door opened and Father Sanchez bustled in.

"What's this, Quintana?" demanded the little round priest of the lean one. "I thought we agreed to cease beating the neophytes for minor infractions."

"Minor!" spouted Quintana. "This little brother," he said with a sneer, "is disrespectful and willfully disobedient. He must be used as an example."

"Yes, but what kind of example will he be?"

"I will not discuss this with you in front of the prisoner and the mayordomo. We may exchange views later. . . . Why did you interrupt me anyway?"

"I came to tell you that Capitan Zuniga is here and wishes to speak with you immediately."

"Why didn't you say so at first?" stormed Quintana, pushing Lazario aside on his way to the door. "You may take over here, and do as you will with this . . . this . . . rebel!"

Sanchez and Lazario removed Donato from the hook and laid him face down on a rough wooden bench. "Bring me the salve from my cell—the blue tin on the shelf," the priest ordered.

When the mayordomo had gone to fetch the ointment, Sanchez sat on the bench beside the huddled form. He tried ever so gently to place a folded cloth beneath Donato's head, but even that slight movement caused a groan to escape the clenched teeth of the neophyte.

"Ah, Donato, my friend," murmured Padre Sanchez, "he will beat you to death next time. He is in charge of discipline, so who can stop him? Why do you persist in sneaking out?"

Bit by bit, in gasps expelled past shudders of pain, Donato told how he had visited the free-roaming Indians who lived in the Temblor range of mountains. There he had met a girl and fallen in love. But her people were preparing to move to their summer hunting grounds, much farther to the north.

"I must see her . . . convince her . . . marry me and

remain here," Donato coughed.

"But why did you not tell us this before? If she is willing to become a Christian, we will welcome her among us."

"Quintana did not . . . believe me . . . said I ran away . . . to sin with the heathen."

"But if she returned with you, that would prove—"

"She would not. She says Christians are too cruel and not to be trusted."

CHAPTER 9

Another mark of how much Will was accepted by the Yokuts came when he was asked to accompany the men on a hunting trip. Falcon's wife examined his wound and pronounced him healed and able to go, and Will was eager to give up the enforced inactivity. Besides, he thought it was about time to help replenish the Yokuts' stores that he had been consuming.

Awakened well before dawn by Blackbird, the boy excitedly informed Will that he was also invited on this hunt. Coyote had been selected to lead the group of four and Falcon would remain in camp. Will was without a rifle, of course, but he was a decent shot with a bow and had been honored to carry Falcon's for the purpose.

The hunters had sweated and bathed in the gray mists of predawn. More important than cleanliness, they wanted to reduce as much as possible the human scent they would carry to the hunt. The Yokuts felt so strongly about this procedure that they would not touch their weapons until the cold plunge had been completed.

A hasty breakfast of cold acorn meal cake followed the bath and then the four headed northeast out of the village, crossing the stream by a shallow rocky ford. Their plan was to ascend a steep ridge of granite rock that ran down to the river.

On a bench of land about halfway up the ridge, the hunting party stopped for a brief rest. Climbing rapidly to the top of a huge boulder, Blackbird gestured for Will to join him. From this vantage point, Will could see back downstream and the Yokuts' village strung out along the banks. Looking upstream, the canyon was bathed in deep shadows as it pressed up against the wall of the Sierra Nevadas.

Will understood that Blackbird was proud of his home and showing off the Yokuts' domain. If the young boy grew to manhood, he would follow his grandfather to leadership of their clan. The future chief swept his arm in a semicircle from mountain shadows down to the tule bog where the stream disappeared into marsh.

Next he pointed his skinny brown arm toward different marks on the horizon and began reciting a list of names. Will was not certain if the names were those of Yokuts' rancherias or of neighboring tribes.

Apparently satisfied that he had passed his self-imposed test, Blackbird made a last stab of his finger. "Tubatulabal," he said as he hopped down off the rock.

The yellow disk of the sun was climbing above the Sierra, riding on the outstretched arms of the pines on the high ridges, when the hunters began their stalk. The breeze off the peaks was dying down, but its faint trace still bore the chill of the snowy summits and the tang of the mountain cedars.

Coyote and Meho were carrying their deer-head disguises. At a spot where two ravines met, the hunting party separated into two groups. The two Yokut men tied on their animal camouflage gear, explaining that a short distance up the left-hand draw was a spring and a small meadow. The Yokuts had often successfully hunted there before, but it required a painfully slow creeping approach.

Will and Blackbird were instructed to wait a few minutes, then begin moving up the canyon on the right. It was not as likely that deer would be found foraging in the right-hand fork, but Will would be in a position to get a shot if a deer was spooked and came over the ridge.

Will and his small partner squatted down to wait. Blackbird was doing such an intense job of scanning the brush ahead that Will took an opportunity to examine Falcon's bow.

The weapon was made of a stout piece of elderberry branch, smoothly finished. The front was rounded and the face toward the archer was flat. The flat surface was strengthened with an application of deer sinew glued lengthwise, and deer sinew was also used as the bow-strings.

Falcon had also presented Will with pouches of arrow shafts and heads to accompany the bow. Both of these were carried by Blackbird. Over one shoulder he wore a fox-skin quiver containing the feathered willow shafts. Around his neck, hanging on his chest, was a smaller buckskin bag that had different sizes of obsidian heads attached to short willow foreshafts.

In this way the Yokut hunter could quickly change the type of killing point to suit the game being sought, and if the arrowhead broke off in a wound, the main shaft could be recovered. When Will extended his hand toward the small boy, Blackbird immediately knew what was wanted. He carefully selected the straightest and best-feathered shaft and coupled it to a newly made obsidian head.

Will nocked the arrow and practiced bringing it to a

full draw. He thought it wise to imitate the Yokuts' stance with the bow held at an angle to the left across the front of his body. The trapper nodded his readiness to proceed.

The tall, sun-bronzed white man and the short, dusky Indian child made their way up the right-hand draw. Will was amused to see the caution with which Blackbird took each step, placing his bare foot carefully and stopping after each pace to watch and listen.

There had been no sound from the direction the other hunters had taken, so Will was agreeable to the slow advance adopted by Blackbird. The trapper did not want to range past the location of the other two and let the quarry sneak out behind them.

A file of quail paraded across in front of them. Several birds took turns hopping up on a prominent rock to inspect the humans before proceeding. The Yokuts made a small arrowhead with projecting prongs for stunning birds, but they also had means of trapping quail in larger numbers.

When the last quail had scurried off into the chaparral, Will and Blackbird approached the stone perch. Above them on one side was a tangle of buckeye limbs and trunks. Several of the trees had blown down in the winter's storms, but with the enthusiasm always shown by buckeyes, the remaining twisted limbs were already covered in bright green leaves.

The hillside on their right was occupied with patches of gooseberry bushes. These thickets were showing the dark red buds that precede the outburst of the fruit. Higher up, the slope was dotted with oak trees sprinkled with a few faded green leaves that had neglected to fall the previous autumn.

Marking the open area between gooseberries and oaks were bands of poppies; brilliant orange in several places and sunshine yellow in others. Will struggled to keep his attention on the hunting and off the scenery.

A quail called from the gooseberry thicket closest to the bottom of the ravine. It was answered by another hidden in the mass of buckeye branches and yet another from the growth of oaks. Will's mind did a curious double-voiced response: half his brain was still glorying in the beauty of the scene, while another part was already screaming a warning.

It was fortunate that the warning voice overrode the admiration of the view. Will yelled "Get down!" and pushed Blackbird behind a rock just as a Mojave killing stick whirred past the little boy's ear.

The throw came from the clump of gooseberry bushes only twenty feet away. The desert Indian who had hurled it was already following up the attack, charging toward Will with an upraised knife.

Will knew that the single arrow now nocked would determine whether he lived or died. The little voice also reminded him that, depending on how many other Mojaves went with the quail calls, he might be dead anyway.

This added worry did not interfere with his aim or make him hesitate to release the arrow. The obsidian arrowhead, as sharp as a shard of glass, pierced the warrior's chest and passed almost completely through his body. His feet stumbled over a small tree limb, and he fell face forward on the grassy turf. The arrow point protruded two feet above his backbone.

There was not a second to be spent in self-congratulation. Two equally terrifying screams rose from opposite sides of the canyon. The Mojave high on the slope who had been in the cover of the oak trees broke into the open. The other attacker, waiting in the mass of buckeye branches, loosed an arrow without ever showing himself.

The downhill shot and the interference of the buckeye leaves deflected the arrow's path. It landed between Will's legs and the stone point shattered on the rock beside which Blackbird was crouched. Cooler under fire than many a grown man, the Yokut boy had fitted another broad point to a shaft and was handing it to Will.

Will grabbed the arrow from the child, but also shouted to him, "Run! Run!" and gave the boy a shove. The trapper was too busy lining up his next shot to see the reproachful look on the child's face. Blackbird slipped off the arrow pouches and made a dash back the way they had come.

Will had not fired his second arrow when another came whizzing at him from the buckeye clump. This time the Mojave's aim was true. In fact, it was too good. Directly in line with Will's chest, the arrow struck squarely on Falcon's bow. The arrow point stuck in the elderberry wood and the impact made the bow spring out of Will's hand like a wounded animal jumps when shot.

Will's second arrow discharged wildly into the air, passing high over the attacker's head. The white man knew that he could not survive another shot and he had no time to retrieve the bow. Instead, Will pulled one of the knives from his belt and charged the Mojave.

The startled desert Indian looked up to see Will leaping over a fallen buckeye trunk with a yell of his own and the gleaming knife flashing in his hand.

The Indian made a wild swing with his bow, trying

to stop Will's rush or fend off the knife. The bow and the blade collided, forcing Will's hand wide of its mark. The power of his rush carried him atop the Indian and they tumbled over into the buckeye.

The native's hands closed over Will's wrist, intent on gaining possession of the skinning knife. Will drew back his left arm and drove a clenched fist into the Indian's jaw.

The desert-dweller's head snapped back, but his grasp on Will's knife-hand did not waver. The Indian twisted Will's arm inward, knotting the wrist joint. Again and again Will drove his fist into the Mojave's face. The round-house blows delivered in their tumbling struggle in the brush heap had little effect.

Will's inner voice reminded him of the desperate need to hurry. Only seconds remained before the remaining warrior came down from the oaks and finished the contest forever.

The Mojave was winning the struggle for the knife. The trapper's fingers were numbing and releasing their grip. Will tried again to drive his fist into the Indian's face, but the Indian ducked his head against the blow. Over they rolled again, coming to an abrupt stop against a fallen buckeye trunk with the Mojave uppermost.

A savage gleam of victory appeared in the eyes of the desert tribesman. He sensed that he controlled the blade, and he pushed it downward toward the trapper's throat.

From the direction of the other slope came the sound of running sandled feet. The other attacker was nearly down the hill. Suddenly there was the twang of a bowstring and a piercing cry. This scream was followed by an angry, outraged shout.

Without thinking, the warrior on top of Will spun his head around at the sound. It was just the opportunity Will had needed.

With his free hand the trapper grabbed a buckeye limb and swung it with all his strength against the Indian's head. The heavy branch crashed into the warrior's skull, and he crumbled much as the buckeye trunk had fallen in the winter's wind.

Will threw the Indian from him, and jumped the opposite direction into the thickest cover of the buckeye tangle. As he peered cautiously over the trunk, he saw an astonishing scene.

The last member of the desert-tribe's ambush was advancing to a kill, but not toward the trapper. The third attacker was dressed in a baggy shirt that hung to his knees. He was brandishing a killing stick at Blackbird, who cowered with his back against a boulder. The grimacing warrior was walking awkwardly, limping and halting.

The cause of his crippled movement was the point of a Yokuts' arrowhead buried deeply in his thigh, pinning the smock to his leg. Blackbird had disobeyed Will's order, retrieved his grandfather's bow and shot the enemy!

Will grabbed the fallen Mojave weapon and nocked another arrow. Climbing out from the jumble of brush, the scout shouted, "Hold it right there!"

The wounded Indian did not understand the words, but the sudden English speech from a man he thought wounded or killed jerked him around. Disbelief, anger and pain competed on his face. He slowly dropped his hands to his sides, letting the killing stick fall to the ground. His features were flat, but more startling was the fact that his ears had been cut off next to his head.

"You're not Mojave. Why'd you jump us?" demanded Will.

In a growing stain from the barbed shaft, blood spread down the man's smock in a fan shape. He stood awkwardly, all his weight on his good leg.

"Please, señor," he said in clear Spanish, "you will help me remove the arrow?"

"First, I want some answers. Where'd you come from?"

"My name is Paco. I am—was a neophyte of the Mission Santa Barbara. I ran away from the mission and the Mojaves took me in. Please, sir, can you help me?"

"That still doesn't explain why you helped these sons of perdition attack us."

"But I did not, señor. I shot no arrow. I threw no club."

"You didn't come charging down the hill to wish me good luck. Blackbird here saved my life by nailing you."

The mission Indian hung his head. "It is true, what you say. But the fierce ones of the desert demanded I must prove myself true to them or they would kill me! They said a spy of the Mexicans was here and that attacking would revenge the wounding of their chief." The blood stain had spread to the hem of the smock and begun to drip on the ground. The man visibly paled and swayed.

"Wounding? He's not dead?"

"No, señor. Sihuarro is recovering his strength. His brother, the shaman, argues that Sihuarro was not defeated really. His spirit only sojourned in the land beyond, gathering power to return and defeat all Mexicans, all foreigners."

"So that is the reason for this raid? Sihuarro could prove it was true by having me killed?"

"Please, señor, may I sit down?"

Will made no reply, nor did he lower the arrow point from its aim at Paco's belly.

"Yes, yes," pleaded the man. "What you say is true. Sihuarro said that the raiders would kill you without difficulty and without causing war with the Yokuts."

At last Will gestured with a shake of the arrow point for the Indian to sit. Paco crumpled more than sat, catching himself only on his elbows before he fell completely flat.

Blackbird ran to Will and without saying a word grabbed the trapper around the legs and hugged him tight. Will was astonished for an instant, then reached down and tousled the boy's shaggy mop of hair.

"You did well, Blackbird. You saved my life."

"I was scared," the boy blurted out. "I thought you were getting killed, then I thought I was and . . . I never shot a man before . . ." his voice trailed off. He made no sobbing noise, but a silent tremor went through his body.

"But you did well . . . you were brave," encouraged Will. "Not many would have found the courage to return."

"I began to run," Blackbird said with a great sigh, "then I remembered: I will be chief someday."

———

Moments later Coyote and Meho came over the ridge and descended to an amazing sight. They found Will bandaging the leg of an unconscious mission Indian while Blackbird gathered a collection of Mojave weapons from two dead warriors.

CHAPTER 10

On a small knoll, clear of the surrounding willows, Falcon looked toward the west. He shaded his eyes against the glare of the westering sun, now turning an angry orange as it descended.

Will stood without speaking alongside the old man. At last the chief volunteered, "I look for sign of Meho's return."

"Yes," agreed the scout, "he said he would be back the same day he went to gather flint rocks."

That had been two days ago. When the toolmaker's lateness had first been noted, everyone said he must have found game to his liking. But now no one spoke of him at all. It was as if the Yokuts wanted to avoid thinking about what might have happened to him.

Falcon muttered something low, almost to himself. It sounded like, "The West has taken him."

Will observed quietly, respectful of the old man's thoughts, "Should we not search for him?"

Falcon rounded on him suddenly and spoke sharply, "No! The West has taken him. We will not speak of it further."

———

"I must leave you," Will said in his best Yokuts'

speech. He was addressing a council of Yokut elders headed by Falcon. The men were dressed formally in their buckskin vests trimmed with fur and bits of shell.

Falcon spoke. "But why, our brother of the reeds? You have shown yourself to be truehearted and brave. Why would you separate yourself from us?"

"Because, Father," said Will with respect, "as long as I remain here, your people cannot have peace with the Mojaves. I endanger your families. Blackbird might have been killed for being with me. I cannot permit this."

Falcon stood erect on the side of the fire opposite Will and waited politely for him to finish. The Indian's hair was tied into two braids and laced with milkweed string twisted with eagle down. "I would say that I owe you the life of my grandson. You are welcome to live with my household forever. If need be we will fight the Mojaves together."

Coyote followed in turn, pleading with Will to remain. Others of the clan took turns expressing their willingness to face the threat of the desert tribe if the white man would remain.

Finally, Will alone stood before the silent, expectant group. A chunk of burning oak broke and crumbled in the fire pit, tiny sparks flying up. He shook his head gravely. "My father and my brothers and my friends . . . I owe you very much . . . but I cannot remain now. I came to this land for the purpose of furs. Now I have no means to continue *that* purpose, but I have not yet found another. What is more, I must seek news of my white brothers, if any of them still live. I must go."

Among the Yokuts, when a man expressed his decision after taking council, there was no more discussion, no continued debate. It was settled and Falcon rose to confirm the choice.

"So," the silvery-haired chief declared, "our brother Sequoyah will go from us. Let us smoke to bless his going." A short-stemmed clay pipe already charged with native tobacco was lit with a coal from the fire. Falcon blew smoke to the four points of the compass, and toward the sky. He then passed the pipe to Will who repeated the motion, then returned it. The small tube of fragrant embers was passed around the circle, and came back to Falcon again.

From around his neck, Falcon drew a string of the fuzzy red topknots of the mountain woodpeckers. It was one of the most precious things the Yokuts possessed and a mark of Falcon's status. "Take this, my son," he offered. "We know the Mexicans esteem it not, but should you wander among others of the Yokuts, they will know you for a man of honor and importance. Also, you must take my bow as your own."

Will thanked Falcon for this kindness and the meeting was over. The council began to disperse to their huts, but Coyote drew Will aside.

"There is yet one more matter to speak of," explained Coyote, tugging on a braid. "Since you spared the life of the man Paco, what do you wish done with him?"

Will had already considered this. "I would have allowed him to return to the Mojaves, but he was afraid. I know you do not trust him and cannot permit him to remain with you, so my way is clear."

"Good," nodded Coyote, "send him away to walk alone. His cropped ears mark him as a thief. Every hand will be turned against him wherever he goes."

"That was not my meaning," corrected Will. "I will

take him with me. I have explained that he has no choice."

"You are wrong," Coyote argued. "He will knife you as you sleep."

"I think not," shrugged Will, "but I will be wary. Perhaps I will be back this way again soon and we will see who was right."

Coyote shook his head and snorted a mocking chuckle. "If you are wrong, my brother, you will not return this way ever."

CHAPTER 11

The morning came for Will to take his leave of the Yokuts and cross the great central valley and the coastal range of mountains. A three-day journey separated the Yokuts' nation from Spanish California.

The scout awoke in the predawn grayness to the faint flutter of a rising east wind. The camp was perfectly still. Far off he heard a jay scolding some other creature for waking him so early. Closer by, the creek laughed and gurgled as it lapped against the roots of a thirsty willow.

Gazing up at the reed-thatched ceiling took Will back to the hut in which he had been imprisoned by the Mojaves. The similarity lasted only a moment though; the Yokuts' village was too peaceful for such a disturbing comparison to last. The sense of calm and belonging carried Will's thoughts toward a dimly remembered childhood home on the Mississippi.

The trapper rolled over in the rabbitskin blanket. He was so wrapped up in memories that the fact that Blackbird was missing took a minute to register. The boy's sleeping cover was thrown in a corner of the hut and he was gone.

Will shook off the pleasant sleepiness and pulled himself awake. Where had the boy gone and why? Blackbird knew that the scout was leaving. Why would he choose this morning to disappear?

Exiting his hut, Will began a mental list of the more likely places to search. For a few steps Blackbird's footprints showed plainly in the cleared area around the huts. Will followed them quietly, not wanting to rouse the camp. The trail was lost after a few paces in the jumble of tracks around the village.

Down at the sweathouse? wondered Will. The communal structure next to the creek was deserted this early in the morning. Will did not need to feel the ashes; the cool temperature inside told him that the hut had not been used since the previous day.

The trapper searched the dark-green gooseberry thickets for signs that Blackbird might have gone in search of breakfast. He found no trace of the eight-year-old until he came to the trail that they had followed into the Mojave ambush.

Discovering the next footprint, he knew that he was on the right track. In fact, he already knew the destination.

Ignoring the faint traces of the young boy's passing, Will cut cross-country toward a rocky bluff that stood out against the skyline. It was the same spot where he and Blackbird had surveyed the Yokuts' world.

———

"Take me with you." Blackbird made the demand without any preamble as the scout joined him on the stony ledge.

"I can't do that," answered Will. "I don't know what I'll find or how I'll be received, and I sure won't chance your life to find out."

"But you are going west, and I will never see you again," mourned the boy, his brown eyes searching Will's face. "It makes my heart hurt. First my mother, then my father, and now you. Take me with you."

The scout gently explained. "But what about your grandfather? He needs you, and your people need you. Besides, it's not as you've said. I'm headed west, but I'm not going to die. I'll be back this way soon."

"How can I know that you are speaking the truth?" questioned the child. "No other one who has gone west has returned."

Will thought for a moment, then drew one of the Green River knives from the leather straps that crossed the front of his buckskin jacket.

"Look," he said, "I want you to keep this. I will hold its twin. Whenever you use it or see it, you must think of me and I will do the same of you. Keep it safe, because it and its brother-knife must be reunited before the snow flies in the passes." The scout gestured toward the high mountains to the east. "Learn all you can from your grandfather about the ways of the wilderness. Soon enough, you will be of an age to join me as a scout."

"Sequoyah," said the boy, "there is evil in the West. Come again soon, before it swallows you."

The child would not return to the camp. Instead, he remained at his post, gazing out toward the path that led toward the ocean, following his friend with his eyes and lifting him with his heart.

———

"I wish you would not do this, señor," asserted Paco for the third time in as many minutes.

Will had been trying to ignore the pleading mission

Indian, but decided he could not stand listening to it for another minute, let alone days.

The scout whirled around, the fringe on his buckskin leggings twirling. "For the last time, Paco, you have no choice, unless you want me to let you wander off to starve. Why are you afraid?"

"You do not understand, señor. If I go back, they will beat me to death."

"Bah," snorted Will. "You're not serious. If you go back of your own free will, they probably won't beat you at all."

"Listen to me, señor," begged the Indian, who was leaning heavily on a crutch made of mountain mahogany. "Perhaps you are right about the holy fathers, but they are not the ones who will punish me. They are not the men who did this." The short, stocky man stopped moving and forced Will to turn and look.

"Capitan Zuniga, he cut off my ears and this time he will cut out my heart."

"Paco, if you got your ears trimmed, it's only because you are a thief."

"No, no, señor. That is what Capitan Zuniga told the fathers so they would not trust me, but it is not so."

Will gestured impatiently for Paco to start walking again and the two men resumed their march. They were skirting the southern end of the great valley's tule bog. Over his shoulder Will demanded to know the real reason for their cruel punishment if Paco was not a thief.

"Ah, señor. It is what I heard Capitan Zuniga and Don Dominguez plotting. They intend to push the governor to take over the mission lands. I tried to tell the fathers this, but Capitan Zuniga said I was lying to cover up my thievery."

"It sounds pretty fanciful to me also," commented the scout. "Let it go for now and I'll speak up on your behalf if need be. Now fill me in on the mission. What's it like?"

They camped that night in Canyon de las Uvas. Will noticed the steep hillsides covered with wild grapevines, giving the canyon its name.

Over a supper of roast rabbit shot by Will and acorn meal cakes provided by the Yokuts, Paco gave the young trapper a sketch of life in Spanish California.

"I was born at the mission," he began. "My grandparents were of the Chumash people living at a rancheria right where Presidio Santa Barbara now stands. They lived off the sea, fishing and gathering. They made shell money and traded it with other people for things they needed.

"When the holy fathers came, everything changed. The Spaniards invited my grandparents' people to come to the mission. They were not forced to become Christian, but the holy fathers told them stories about how the Lord Jesus died for their sins and they listened. They were told that if they became neophytes they would receive clothing, better food, homes, be taught to grow crops."

"So they wanted to join the mission?" asked Will.

"Si, but they had to agree to many things. If they became neophytes, they had to work for the padres and no longer could they leave without permission."

"And runaways are forced to return and are punished?" Will inquired.

"That is right. Sometimes my people tried to revolt. My father died in one such attempt. But he was not a rebel, señor. He was killed protecting the mission from others who wanted to burn it down."

"Surely your people outnumber the Spaniards many times over," offered Will, remembering his grandfather's stories about the American Revolution against the British. "Why didn't they—what's that noise?"

A low rumbling sound could be heard in the distance. Very faint at first and harmless, like the drumming of rain on his cabin roof back on the Mississippi, the sound swelled until it resembled a continuous roll of thunder instead of a gentle rain. The noise seemed to be sweeping toward them, down from the high pass.

The rumble increased in volume and tempo, reminding Will of an avalanche heard in the heights of the Rockies. He jumped to his feet. "I know that sound," he exclaimed. "It's a buffalo stampede. I saw one when we were crossing the plains." Unconsciously he switched to speaking English in his excitement. "This oak here is good and stout. Quick, up . . ."

Paco still sat by the fire. "Calm yourself, señor," he urged. "There are no buff . . . what did you say, 'bufflers'? There are none here."

"Then what?" demanded Will.

A herd of horses swung into moonlit view. Their leader, a glossy black stallion of immense size, swept around a rocky outcropping two hundred yards away.

At the sight of the campfire, the stallion did not even break stride. He led his band in a great s-curve that carried them to the farthest side of the canyon opposite the two men.

Will caught brief glimpses of various horse hides— dark, light, pinto and spotted—as he stood watching the spectacle. Like the sudden release of a river hitting the rim of a waterfall, the horse herd spilled past the camp. Eyes flashing in the light of the moon, their hooves churned the sage into a piercingly sharp fragrance that filled the night air, and then they were gone.

Will stood staring after them. From behind him the still-seated Paco spoke, "There you see a part of the answer, señor."

"Answer—what answer?" said Will, who had forgotten his question.

"You asked why my people and the other Indios did not throw out the Spaniards. It is true that they came with weapons and armor of iron and with gunpowder. But most of all, they came with horses from whom these wild ones descend. With such beasts they can move men and supplies in great numbers and so quickly."

"Well why don't your people learn to ride—meet the Spanish as equals? You could catch that one herd and have mounts for seventy-five or one hundred men."

Paco looked furtive for an instant; the expression of a weasel surprised in the hen house. "Oh no, señor," he said quickly and shook his head, "only *gente de razón*, the people of reason, are permitted to become caballeros. It is forbidden for any of my people to even get on a horse."

CHAPTER 12

Don Pedro Rivera y Cruz stood on the veranda of his hacienda and watched his gardener hoeing weeds. Don Pedro's thoughts drifted back some twenty-five years earlier to a tiny garden outside the adobe walls of Presidio Santa Barbara.

The Rivera y Cruz family was of noble blood, well-known and highly regarded in Spain. But notoriety and nobility, even combined with a Jesuit education, could not ensure wealth and position on the future adult lives of thirteen children. As the tenth in line, Don Pedro's military career in the Americas had been decided long before he wore his first beard.

The ranchero rubbed his hand over his now clean-shaven face, and then, by habit, up over his balding head. He thought ruefully how thick and black his hair had been when he was a young cuero, a leather-jacket soldier.

With his good looks and confident manner, there had been no difficulty convincing lovely Guadalupe Flores to become his bride. They were married in the Presidio chapel during the first month of the year 1801. She was the first to tend the scrap of garden outside the wall of the fort, and she was in his thoughts now.

Don Pedro's military service might have been without distinction had it depended on fighting battles. Garrison duty in California was almost always peaceful.

But in a different way, Don Pedro had earned the gratitude of Spain. In 1812 both the presidio and the mission were destroyed by a cataclysmic earthquake. Don Pedro put his studies from his youth to good use. Demonstrating an amazing skill at architecture and engineering, he soon had rebuilt both structures and it was recognized far and wide that the buildings were better than the originals.

At his retirement from military service, he had received a grant of land and set to work stocking it with cattle. At first there had been little profit in the sale of meat and tallow, but in time the demand for rawhide drew attention to California.

Within ten years, the first hesitant attempts at commerce with America's eastern states had grown into an active, thriving business. Valued at two dollars apiece, cowhides soon became known as "California banknotes." Their proprietors became wealthy men as the young and energetic United States continued to demand more leather for shoes, boots, saddles and harnesses.

There was only one sadness in the life of the ranchero: His wife had only had one year to share the hacienda built from the profits of his trade, and then she died.

Don Pedro was recalled from his reverie by the sound of creaking saddle leather at the front of the house. Turning the corner of the veranda, he saw that his son was mounted on the bay horse with the white blaze, and was awaiting instructions.

"Ricardo, I want you to ride out to the south pasture and see how the roundup, the rodeo, is going. The last two hundred hides are cured and stacked. It is time for us to prepare more."

"Si, Father," replied the slim young man. His features duplicated those of his sister Francesca, but in a chiseled, masculine way. He controlled the prancing bay horse easily and took the time to secure under his chin the strap of his flat crowned hat.

Don Pedro Rivera y Cruz looked at his son with pride. "Before your return tomorrow, ride up Canyon Perdido. I have had a report that some of our cows have been slaughtered there."

The son turned the bay in a circle back toward Don Pedro, the silver conchos on the tack flashing in the sunlight. "Should I take some men with me, Father?"

"No, not till we know more. It is probably the work of some travellers or Indios. Anyway, if it is only one or two dead animals and they have left the hides, it does not matter. We will not begrudge anyone meat, so long as they are respectful. Vaya con Dios, my son."

Ricardo had only to touch the bay's flanks with the tips of the five-inch rowels of his spurs and off they flew. Horse and rider merged into the fluid motion of water bubbling over rocks in a stream bed. In no more than a minute they were out of sight.

Don Pedro again reached up and wiped his work-thickened hand over his bald head with its fringe of short white hair. How proud his wife would have been of their two almost-grown children and how fine the rancho had become.

"Miguel," he called to the rancho gardener, "are the strawberries ripe yet? Ah, no matter, bring some anyway, the ripest you can find." To himself he sighed, "She could never wait for them to get really ready. Besides, she always said there was something magic about the first strawberries of spring." Don Pedro shook off his thoughts and turned to climb the steps back to his office.

CHAPTER 13

Will and Paco worked through the mountains on a path that wound its way past forests of oaks and pinyon pines. On the trail they came to a deserted village in a hilly canyon.

Will stopped to examine the forlorn site. A circle of collapsed reed huts encircled by a mud wall was all that was left. On a bluff above the village were some grinding holes bored into a granite slab and the remains of a rectangular foundation.

The trapper called Paco over to him. "What about this? I never saw the Yokuts build anything that wasn't round."

Paco studied the ground for a moment. Next, he squinted down at a corner of the green valley that could be seen through the canyon's mouth. A sheen of silver reflected a large lake's presence in the valley.

"This place I have never been to before, but I have heard of it. There was once a great Yokuts' village here. The holy fathers came to this place and built a small mission. That must be the foundation. This was many years before I was born.

"Then some runaways passed through here, fleeing from Mission Santa Barbara. The military commander used this place as a fort to attack the tribes that were hiding the huidos, the runaways.

"When the Yokuts protested, he punished them also, so they all moved away and never returned. Soon the padres went away too."

Will nodded his understanding and tried to imagine what life might have been like here. "So the commander, by being so hard, chased away those that the priests had come here to seek. He made their work more difficult, not easier."

There was nothing to add to that. But it gave Will much to think about as the two pushed on upward through passes that led toward Santa Barbara. Eventually they faced a high rounded ridge covered in dark green grass and dotted with oaks.

"Just across those mountains, señor." The mission Indian directed Will's gaze to a zigzag path of red dirt, streaking the hillside like a faded scar over an old wound.

———

The next morning they were up before sunrise. Will was eager to cross the threshold of Spanish California. He had heard stories about the richness of the mission lands and their exotic Spanish culture from a handful of English-speaking trappers who had been there before him. He had seen nothing that resembled civilization in the usual sense of the word since leaving Missouri, a thousand miles and another lifetime ago.

The rounded ridge did not look threatening, but it was steep. The path they followed was long in reaching the top as it plunged in and out of canyons and gorges.

When the scout and the mission Indian finally reached the crest of the hill, Will was out of breath. Paco's leg was aching and he was ready to rest also.

Will looked back the way they had come, thinking how glad he was that the climb was behind them. He was not yet ready to look down the western slope. So many ranges had been crossed only to find another, and still another, and yet another looming ahead, so his enthusiasm to see what lay beyond had been tempered.

It was a shock past anything he had ever experienced to look out from his perch and see ocean! The land dropped away sharply below him, flattening out to a narrow coastal plain just in front of a line of white sand and foaming breakers.

The coastline made an arc, and Will could see it was a bay of sorts. The mountain range on which he stood curved to plunge abruptly into the ocean some miles south of him, while to the north it faded into a rocky point in the dim distance.

Will could see islands across a narrow channel of blue water. One especially clear lay directly before him. The length of its silhouette and the shape of its peaks and valleys showed that it was not inconsequential in size.

Paco tugged at Will's elbow when he saw the scout staring across the water. "My people once lived there," he said.

"There? You mean on that island?"

"Si. It is called Santa Cruz . . . the island of the holy cross. When the Spaniards came to this coast, one made a stop there. A priest lost a valuable silver cross while they were exploring. An ancestor of mine swam out to stop them from leaving so that the cross could be returned. The Spaniards were very impressed and grateful and decided to name the island to honor the event."

Will's first view of the ocean—in fact, of any ocean—filled him with wonder but was overshadowed by a sense of unease. There had never been a time when he had stood on the shore of a lake so vast that he could not see the farther shore. It strained his belief as well as his eyes that no matter how hard he peered into the distance, there was no trace of land. He had the same feeling of disquiet when he had left the little trading post outside Vicksburg: adrift with no farther shore in sight.

He was grateful for the islands on the near horizon. They were like a wall holding back the unutterable loneliness of the sea beyond.

"Come, señor," interrupted Paco. "Let us descend. Santa Barbara is just across these hills."

CHAPTER 14

The California morning was perfect and young Ricardo Rivera y Cruz had enjoyed it to the full. His canter to the cattle roundup was made under brilliantly blue skies and billowy white clouds. He was pleased with the figure he made and with the performance of the horse he had trained.

Passing a group of Indians hired from the mission to repair an irrigation ditch, Ricardo was saluted respectfully. There was no hint of the sullenness that often accompanied their response to other masters.

Ricardo also met a carreta occupied by the daughters Gonzalez. The wooden-wheeled cart was creaking its way toward the market. Old man Gonzalez was not a great ranchero, but he was very successful at raising beauties for marriage. Ricardo touched the brim of his hat as he cantered by, pretending not to notice the giggling that erupted.

Ricardo wondered if one of the Gonzalez sisters might one day be his mate. He had known since he was little that his father had arranged a marriage for him, but he had not been told with whom.

At the age of nineteen, he was not expected to know his future wife. Indeed, decisions about his life were still his father's to make. He had not even been allowed to begin shaving until he was eighteen, and then only with his father's permission.

Thoughts about his own eventual wedding brought his sister to mind. Three years older than Ricardo, at twenty-two, Francesca was six years past the accepted marriage age. Her betrothed, a forty-year-old Don in San Diego, had died in a fall from a horse when Francesca was only fourteen. Some said he was drunk when it happened.

While a hundred other prospective sons-in-law could have been found, the death of Francesca's mother less than a year after her fiance had made Don Pedro reluctant to push her to marry. Don Pedro was proud of his son, but he doted on his daughter.

Ricardo shrugged, glad he was not responsible to find a husband for his sister, and rode into camp.

The roundup concluded smoothly the following morning. The ranch foreman and his vaqueros had gathered about two hundred of the rangy cows into a small meadow. With its surrounding thickets of brush and a rocky stream across one side, it was an ideal holding ground.

Some of the vaqueros were Indians. They were permitted to ride for Don Pedro only after he had applied to the government in Mexico City and was granted a special allowance. It had taken two years and much wrangling, but the prohibition against Indians on horseback had been partially lifted.

After a brief final talk with the foreman, Ricardo concluded that all was going well. By the next evening the cattle would be driven down to a section of the rancho near the ocean where the skinning would take place.

It did not matter that a few neighbor cattle had been

rounded up with Don Pedro's. They would be skinned with the rest and the hides cured, then the finished product returned to the rightful owner.

This approach saved the effort of rounding up those cattle again later, as well as trying to separate out the strays. Since all the rancheros operated the same way, no one was cheated.

The ride up Canyon Perdido took Ricardo away from the ranching and farm operations and away from the travelled roads. The canyon's gnarled oak trees and tangles of brush had a wild, uncivilized appearance, though it was just beyond the sight of the grazing herds.

Ricardo had searched the canyon for strays many times. A path of sorts wound through a boulder-strewn gulch and up the slope toward the mountains. The path was said to eventually climb into the Santa Ynes Valley, but Ricardo had never ridden along it that far.

The bay shied suddenly and a moment later Ricardo caught the stench of rotting flesh. Around the next bend of the arroyo, he came upon the partially dismembered carcass of a cow.

It was lying next to a rock basin that held a small pool of water. The head and forequarters of the cow were partly covered with a pile of leaves and dirt. Someone had done a poor job of hiding their kill.

The horse's nostrils flared and it snorted violently twice, then pranced in a tight circle. "Easy," said the caballero to the bay, "easy."

Ricardo searched the rocks and the tree branches for a hide. Some wild beast had been feasting on the remains—that was certain. But the cow must have been killed and skinned for its hide.

He never saw the grizzly till it charged. The silver-tipped, hunch-backed bear thought the horse and rider were moving in on his larder, and he was having none of it.

The bay screamed as only a horse that has been frightened near to death can sound. It jumped straight up and lashed out with its hind feet, catching the bear on the nose and momentarily stunning him.

But the grizzly was not easily put off the attack. Lunging again, it closed its jaws over a scrap of the horse's tail and with that tenuous hold pulled the bay backwards.

The horse was truly panicked now, and stood almost straight up and down on its forefeet. The bay's rear hooves pounded against the bear's shoulders, but it hung on grimly.

On the third desperate plunge, Ricardo parted company with the bay and flew off forward. Arcing through the air over the carrion pile, he landed heavily on the rocky basin and was knocked unconscious.

When he came to, he lay very still, taking stock of his injuries before attempting to move. It was the wisest decision he ever made. Only an instant later, the hot, rotten-smelling breath of the grizzly blasted his neck.

In the tug of war with the stallion, the silver-tipped beast had come away with only a mouthful of horse tail for all his trouble. Knocked cross-eyed from the blow to his skull and smarting from the drumming his shoulders had taken, the bruin was still spoiling for a fight. He swung his slavering muzzle from side to side, his damaged nose having trouble separating the strong man scent from the smell of the escaped horse and the odor of the decaying cow.

Ricardo felt the bear snuffling along his legs. The

young man's mind was racing with horrifying possibilities. Even if he convinced the grizzly he was dead, what if the bear decided to add him to the carrion pile?

That chilling nightmare became a bloody reality when the humpback suddenly closed his jaw over Ricardo's head and sank his razor-sharp teeth to the bone. Ricardo let out a yell almost equal to the bay's.

The bear dropped him, confused. A deep, angry growl rumbled like an earthquake from the depths of the beast.

In the split second that elapsed between the grizzly's surprise and its decision to tear the man-thing into bloody pieces, an obsidian arrowhead sliced into its neck.

Ricardo scrambled for his life. Playing dead was now out of the question; he was only seconds away from the reality.

With one hand he held his pierced and torn scalp, bleeding from half a dozen deep gashes. With the other hand he dragged himself over the rocks, crying with terror and praying that he would not pass out.

Will Reed nocked another arrow as the grizzly sat up on its haunches, roaring. It swatted clumsily at the painful barb sticking in its neck.

The shaft broke off and the bear drove the point inward, sending the creature into a rage of pain. The second arrow struck low on the flank, and the bear dropped its great head to bite at its own side.

Closing its teeth over the barbed shaft and ripping it free of flesh, the silver-tip stood erect. Flashing eyes searched for the source of the cruel flying things.

The grizzly spotted Will standing next to a tree at the edge of the clearing and bellowed at him, challenging him. "I am the master here," he roared. "No one disputes the ground I own and lives to tell of it."

Will fumbled in the pouch for another arrowhead. His hand closed over one, drew it out—too small! The tiny flake of stone was only fit for killing rabbits, not this berserk hulk of killing ferocity.

He scrabbled through the pouch again, coming up with another only a little larger. Across the stone basin Will could see Ricardo scrambling up a rocky ledge to safety. Time to think about his own safety.

"Paco," Will called. "Paco, distract him! Throw a rock, something!" There was no answer; the Indian was long gone.

The bear's claws rattled the granite as he dropped to all fours, ready to charge. This contest was about to end!

A quick glance upward—no tree limbs near the ground—no time to run—no way to the safety of the rocks. Go down fighting.

Will drew out one last arrow shaft as the bear rushed, fitted the barb to the socket, nocked the arrow, and released.

The last arrow, a mere pinprick, also lodged in the thick folds of the bear's neck. The beast, on him now, seized the bow in its teeth, tearing it from him.

One more swat of an enormous paw at this latest nuisance, then the human was to be crushed. The grizzly batted hurriedly at the latest arrow, striking again the first barb whose shaft just protruded from the long, coarse hair, and driving it home.

The five-inch-long shard of razor-sharp black glass, pushed by a ton of angry grizzly, sliced through the bear's carotid artery. Blood burst from the wound, spraying the silver-tipped fur with crimson.

The bear collapsed like a huge fur sack full of air that

had been suddenly punctured. The grizzly's lips were still curled back from his fangs, and on either side of the massive jaws lay shattered pieces of Falcon's bow.

The terror of the canyon lay silently in a heap at Will's feet.

But Will knew there was no time to relish this unlikely victory. Turning to climb the rock face Ricardo had crawled up, he found the horseman cradling his lacerated head in both hands. Blood streamed over and between his fingers, staining his hands and face scarlet.

The young man's breath was coming in ragged gasps, and he did not try to look up when Will approached.

"Can you hear me?" Will asked gently in Spanish.

"Si, and I think I owe you my life," Ricardo choked between gasps.

"Just sit easy until I find something to bind you up with. We've got to get you some help fast. You're losing too much blood."

Will tore a strip off the Spaniard's linen shirt. "Take your hands down now," he instructed.

Slowly, reluctantly, Ricardo did as he was told. Will saw why the injured man had been holding on so tightly: his scalp was bitten completely through in places. White bone gleamed dully against crimson streaks. The scalp was nearly detached around half the circle of the grizzly's bite. Ricardo's face visibly slipped, his features wrinkling grotesquely.

Trying to keep the wounded man from seeing him shudder, Will worked swiftly to wrap the scalp with linen. Searching for the least injured place he could find, Will knotted the bandage there and prayed the bleeding would stop.

Will had to guide Ricardo's booted feet into the

cracks in the rock in order for the mauled man to climb back down. Reaching the bottom, the trapper brought the young horseman a drink of water from the pool.

"I'll fix you as comfortable as I can," said Will. "I'm a stranger here, so I need you to tell me the quickest route to get help."

"No need, señor," replied Ricardo, "just let me catch my breath and perhaps you can get me one more drink of that excellent water."

When Will had done so, Ricardo placed two fingers against his tongue and blew a shrill whistle. "Aiiee," he winced, "I never knew whistling to hurt before!"

A few moments passed and the bay horse trotted back into the clearing. Lather covered his neck and flanks and his eyes were wild, but he came obediently at his master's signal.

"Do you want me to walk and lead him?" asked Will.

"Not necessary. Lorenzo can carry both of us, and he knows the way home."

Assisting Ricardo into the high-cantled saddle, Will then mounted behind him.

"If you can take the reins, señor, I think perhaps I will concentrate on not falling off again," he said to Will.

Although it had slowed, blood was still flowing from the lacerations and dripping from Ricardo's matted hair.

"Señor, if it is far to your home, then we should seek help sooner," observed Will, keeping a tight grip on the reins to prevent the keyed-up stallion from racing down the faint trail.

A weak voice haltingly responded, "Turn the bay . . . at the fork . . . the mission is just . . ." Then Ricardo's voice faded out altogether.

But Will had heard all that was necessary. He settled

himself firmly, gripping with his knees, and wrapped one arm around the now unconscious rider.

"Come on, Lorenzo," he urged. "Move out." The long-legged bay stretched out his neck and doubled his speed.

Just over the crest of a small hill, the horse broke free of the surrounding brush. Less than a mile below them to the west was the whitewashed mission. Its single bell tower glistened white against the green landscape and the blue of the ocean beyond.

Will rode directly up to the steps of the mission. Small adobe houses and thatched huts crowded the square in front of the great church. It was midafternoon and the square was nearly empty.

The clattering entrance of Lorenzo and the spectacle of the buckskin-clad stranger holding tightly to the bloodied body caused instant commotion. People poured into the square from every direction, then someone rang an alarm bell, as they did for a pirate attack or a fire.

A gray-haired man dressed in the cowled gray robe of a Franciscan padre hurried down the front steps of the mission. At the sight of Ricardo's waxy complexion caked with gore, the priest crossed himself and cried out, "What has happened? Who has murdered poor Ricardo?"

"A grizzly, Father. But he's still alive," explained Will. "Please help me ease him down."

The priest called two neophyte Indians to assist him and the three gently received Ricardo's limp body. As they moved quickly around the side of the building, the priest called back over his shoulder, "We have an infirmary. Follow us."

Will stepped from the horse and looked around for someone to hold the bay. A young boy approached and offered to care for Lorenzo.

In front of the mission was a fountain bubbling with clear water. Will decided that what he needed more than the infirmary was a quick wash and a long drink.

Stepping over to the pool, he washed Ricardo's blood from his hands and face with double handfuls of water. Once the filth was cleansed away, Will bent over the fountain and drank deeply.

When he stood upright, he saw that everyone in the square was staring at him with undisguised curiosity. Neophytes in short tunics like that worn by Paco were standing in groups, evidently discussing him. At a long tank fed by the outflow of the fountain, mission women stopped their laundry chores to gaze. Across the square, a mixed group of soldiers and men dressed in short jackets and tight pants were pointing at him and gesturing. A dark-skinned priest in a gray robe stared for a minute, then hurried away from the mission.

For the first time in a long while, Will was embarrassed. He was grateful when one of the Indians who had helped carry Ricardo returned and approached him. "Father Sanchez asks if you are wounded also? He wants you to come."

"No, I'm all right," responded Will. "But I would like to see how . . . what did the priest call him? How Ricardo is doing."

CHAPTER 15

"Please, allow me to pour you some more wine," Father Sanchez offered.

"No, thanks," responded Will. "It beats anything I ever tried before though. Did you have it brought by ship?"

The pudgy friar chuckled, "Only if you mean the rootstock. We made this wine from grapes grown on our own sunny hillsides." The priest poured himself another glassful and sipped with an appreciative pride. "We are trying other varieties of grapes as well, but I think this will rival any zinfandel in the world."

As Will sat back from the linen-covered dining table, an Indian servant whisked away his empty dinner plate and another removed the silver serving tray bearing the remains of a joint of mutton.

The trapper glanced down at his stained buckskin clothes. Even washed, wrung out and dried, they still smelled of woodsmoke and carried the stains of hunting, fighting and overland journeying. Since arriving at the mission that afternoon, Will had cleaned up and shaved, but his unruly thatch of hair and travel-weary clothing embarrassed him here.

"You live very well," observed Will.

"It is surprising isn't it, here on the edge of the

world?" replied Father Sanchez. "Of course I am just the inheritor of great men of faith like Fathers Serra and Garces. When they arrived, they had to live in reed huts, just like the Indians. Can you imagine that? But look what has been achieved in less than sixty years."

"What about the Indians, Father?" prompted Will as a servant placed a china cup of fragrantly steaming hot chocolate before him.

"Oh, they are such children," laughed the priest. "We have all we can handle constantly checking on them to see if they have followed instructions. They are just as likely to run off and go fishing, but they are good-hearted, simple people.

"We have such a large neophyte population now that we can hire out the young men to the local ranchos for wages."

"What do the workers do with their pay?" inquired Will.

"Bless me," chuckled Father Sanchez. "You don't think such simple ones are responsible enough to handle *money*? Oh no! I meant that their wages are credited to the mission's account, of course, to balance what we purchase in supplies."

"Don't your workers resent giving up all their pay?"

Father Sanchez looked as if this were an astounding thought. "Why should they?" he remarked with surprise. "They receive all the necessities from our hands." He glanced down at his own soft, plump fingers. "No one forced them to become neophytes, señor, and we keep no secrets from them before or after they join our community."

"Isn't it true that most of those young workers are born to Christian families already attached to the mission?"

"That is correct," agreed the padre. "Sadly, the un-believers of the interior are not as receptive as those of the coast."

"I'm not so sure that's true," responded Will. He re-minded the Mexican priest of the interest in Christianity he had seen among the Yokuts. "But there is something else going on as well," he continued. "They seem very suspicious of your people, Father. I understand a very hostile tribe of desert-dwellers is already at war with you."

"You must understand this is a time of confusion," commented Father Sanchez. "We Mexicans have only been free of the yoke of Spain these past ten years. I am Mexican-born, but many of the highest-ranking families like that of Ricardo's father are highly suspect to the Mexican officials.

"Moreover," he continued, "there is much strife in Mexico itself. The military officials have so many con-flicts that they have adopted harsh measures against many tribes. We hope to prosper here in California with-out such difficulties, but who can say?"

The padre's discussion was interrupted by an Indian servant announcing that Captain Zuniga had arrived.

The little priest's round face broke into a frown, the only time during the meal Will had seen him do so. "I wonder what he can want?" muttered Father Sanchez. Turning to Will, he added, "Excuse me a moment, please."

But before the friar could rise from the table, Zuni-ga's lean form and scarred face advanced into the room. He was accompanied by two soldiers wearing bullhide vests and carrying flintlock muskets. This did not look to Will like a friendly visit.

Sanchez tried to be gracious. "Ah, Capitan Zuniga," he began, "may I introduce my guest, Will Reed. He is the trapper from the east who rescued young Rivera."

"The American spy, you mean," said Zuniga abruptly. "Why was he not reported to me immediately? Where are his papers?"

Will answered the questions for himself, trying to smother the instant dislike and hostility he felt. "I only just got here, Capitan. The good Father allowed me to get cleaned up and treated me to a fine dinner. I'm no spy. I was part of a trapping party that was attacked by Mojaves. Captain Beckwith was our leader. He had papers from the governor of Sante Fe, but Beckwith didn't make—"

"Silence," shouted Zuniga. "I have heard enough. I arrest you as a spy. Take him away!" Will was immediately seized by the two soldiers. Zuniga grabbed the necklace of woodpecker topknots and ripped it from Will's neck. The captain ground it under his boot as he followed his captive out the door.

Sanchez protested, "But he saved the boy's life— brought him here to the mission. You can't do this."

The captain turned and remarked coldly, "You had better keep quiet, Father. Harboring a spy is treason and traitors are hanged." He paused to let the point sink in before adding maliciously, "Just like spies."

CHAPTER 16

Will's adobe cell was exactly eight paces long and eight paces wide. After twenty or thirty trips each direction, he could have walked blindfolded and stopped with the tip of his nose one-half inch from the wall.

He actually had been blindfolded and his hands tied behind his back for the march to the cell. These were removed when he was thrust into the prison. There was a tiny window in the stout oak door, but it was already night in Santa Barbara and nothing could be seen.

The tiny room contained a wooden bucket for a chamber pot and a moth-eaten blanket with which to cover the bare earthen floor. That was all.

Will found the blanket by feeling around in the dark, but its prior owners—thousands of fleas—found him the same way. Tossing it to a corner of the cell, he spent the night pacing, thinking, and scratching.

————

"So, Don Jose, now that we have him, what are we going to do with him?" inquired Captain Zuniga.

"For the time being, nothing."

"Nothing!" exploded the hot-tempered captain. "How long do you think it will be before Don Pedro blasts us from Monterrey to Mexico City for imprisoning the man who saved his son? He is still a powerful man and can hurt our plans with Figueroa—perhaps even get me recalled."

The ranchero rocked back and forth on his small feet, a smirk of smug satisfaction on his face. "So, when Don Pedro demands the American's release or else a letter will be sent to the governor, you will obligingly release him."

"But why antagonize Rivera first?"

Zuniga hated the condescension with which Dominguez spoke, but was forced to listen to an explanation that dripped with it. "My dear capitan, you will be at your most politically astute. You will say to Don Pedro, 'So sorry . . . just following orders . . . anxious to please you . . . completely understand.' "

He continued, "Don Pedro will accept your apologies and be mollified at your willingness to see reason, despite your having acted in accordance with written law."

"But what is the point of this charade?" demanded the blunt man of action.

"If we win the confidence of Don Pedro, all is well. If not, well, it gives us something to hold over him."

"You mean—"

"Of course. If need be, the American will be *proven* a spy. And who is it that demanded his release against standing orders? The traitor, Don Pedro Rivera y Cruz."

———

"Careful! Slowly now! Set him down gently!" Francesca Rivera y Cruz saw to it that her brother was carried safely upstairs to his bedroom. Then she took personal charge of tucking him in bed and changing his bandages.

Though she caught her breath at the severity of the gashes in his scalp, she bit her lip and said nothing. Ricardo protested that Father Sanchez had just renewed the compresses before allowing him to go home, but Francesca swallowed the lump in her throat and told her brother to hush and lie still or he'd be going back to the padre. He complied.

When she was convinced that Ricardo was properly attended to, she decided to ride to the mission to thank the good father and the American from the east who had teamed together to save her brother's life.

Francesca called the stableboy, Miquelito, to put her sidesaddle on the buckskin. She had always been too impatient to ride in a slowly creaking carreta anywhere, let alone all the way to Santa Barbara. Off she cantered, leaving her father and aunt to look after Ricardo.

The ride along the curving lanes was a familiar one. Once each week Francesca devoted a day to teaching mission children how to read. Mission policy stated that the children begin work at the looms at the age of nine. Francesca felt that if the neophytes were ever to become gente de razón, people of reason, they needed to be able to read and write.

Although Father Sanchez applauded her assistance, not everyone believed this was a good thing. Some of her father's friends said that education made the Indians think too highly of themselves. Others thought it beneath the dignity of a daughter of an important family to befriend the Indian children. Francesca ignored both opinions, and her father could only shrug his shoulders and reply, "In her heart, she takes after her sainted mother."

As she rode into the dusty plaza in front of the mission, several children were playing near the fountain. Seeing her, they dashed to greet her. "Doña Francesca," they called, "today is not the day for lessons, is it?"

"No, children," she smiled in return, "not today. I will be back on Friday as usual. Where is Father Sanchez?"

The brown-skinned children directed her along the arched colonnade, past the front of the church. Chico, the largest boy of her class, reported having seen the priest enter the mayordomo's quarters on the east side of the mission.

Francesca rewarded Chico by allowing him to hold her horse, which made him immensely proud and the envy of his friends. She hurried to the red-tile-roofed home that stood in the shadow of the bell tower. Reaching its porch, she met Sanchez coming out.

"Ah, Francesca," he called anxiously. "Your brother is doing well? No sudden turn for the worse? He insisted on going home this morning and I agreed against my better judgment. Is he all right?"

"He's fine, Father," she reassured the priest. "I came to thank you for attending him. I also want to thank the man Ricardo tells us saved his life. Where is he? We want to invite him to be a guest in our home."

The chubby padre looked embarrassed and awkwardly shuffled his sandelled feet. "I did not tell Ricardo this morning because I did not want to upset him."

Now it was the girl's turn to be concerned. "Tell him what?" demanded Francesca. "What has happened?"

"The American, Will Reed is his name, has been arrested. Capitan Zuniga came last night and took him to the presidio."

"For what?" exclaimed Francesca. "What has he done?"

"Nothing, to my knowledge. Zuniga says the American is without papers, or something. In fact, I was just going over the day's workplans with our mayordomo and then I intended to ride out to your home to explain this to your father."

"That will not be necessary," blazed Francesca, her eyes flashing dangerously. "I will go home at once and tell him myself!"

CHAPTER 17

Toward dawn Will had dozed off. His weary body had slid down a wall to a seated position, and there he remained as gray light filled the tiny barred window, filtering around the cracks of the door.

The sound of the heavy door creaking on reluctant hinges brought him awake. Jumping to his feet, he found himself staring into the muzzle of a musket. The soldier aiming it told him to back to the opposite wall and not move until the door was shut again.

Will asked several questions of the soldier, but neither he nor his companion made any response. The second soldier set down a wooden bowl and clay jug, then slammed the stout door closed.

The bottle was full of water, for which Will was grateful, but he found it impossible to give thanks for the food.

The bowl contained a mixture of cooked beans and cornmeal with a greasy scum layering the thick mush and drowned weevils floating on the top. A rancid stench attacked Will's nostrils as well. He placed the bowl back down near the door, took the jug of water, and for the second time backed away from the entrance.

Could probably use that stuff to kill the fleas in the blanket, he thought. Once again he fell to brooding about his situation.

He had been attacked by the Mojaves for being an accomplice of the Mexicans. Now the Mexicans figured him for somebody's spy. He berated himself for leaving the Yokuts.

Did this happen to the Good Samaritan, he wondered. *Maybe next time someone's in trouble it should be every man for himself.*

Will had plenty of time to wonder how serious the threat of hanging might be. Of course, if the quality of the fare did not improve, he'd starve to death before they could hang him.

By afternoon, yellow light filled the hole of the door. Taking a deep breath, Will moved the bowl and its noxious contents to the same corner as the vermin-filled blanket.

The opening was only big enough for one eye at a time. Bending down a little, he pressed half his face into it.

He was looking across a dusty courtyard of what was evidently the military garrison. Two soldiers passed, one of them leading a mule. He made out the shadow of a tall pole, perhaps a flag pole, even though he could not see the staff itself.

"Zuniga!" boomed a voice in no-nonsense tones. "Zuniga, where is the American? I want him out now or heads will roll, starting with yours!"

Will could see that the dusty grounds of the presidio had suddenly been stirred into a flurry of activity. A balding man whose muscular size emphasized his obvious anger galloped into the courtyard.

The horse he rode was as black as midnight and he led a fine gray, but the newcomer's face was flushed a deep red that continued over his bald head. The veins of his neck bulged dangerously. Will watched him fling himself from the charger and contemptuously toss the reins to a startled soldier.

The man demanded something of the soldier. Will could only make out another booming, "Zuniga!" Shrinking back from the large man's fury, the soldier pointed a shaking arm over the man's shoulder.

Will glimpsed the captain who had arrested him at the mission advancing into the scrap of his vision. The officer was in full uniform, almost as if he had been expecting this visit.

The volume of the shouted demands fell as the officer made calming gestures. Next the officer nodded his head vigorously and pointed toward Will's cell. The two men turned toward the space where the scout was confined.

Will stepped back against the far wall. A rattle announced that the bolt holding the bar in place across the cell door was pulled free, then the door swung open.

The large man strode directly into the tiny space. "You are the American who saved my son from the grizzly." Don Pedro offered this as a statement, not a question, but Will nodded his head.

"I am Don Pedro Rivera y Cruz," stated the ranchero formally. "I am completely and totally in your debt and have come to see that you are immediately freed."

Don Pedro whirled around to face Captain Zuniga and repeated, "Immediately."

The officer shrugged. "Of course, Don Pedro. As you wish. We were simply following the standing orders for treatment of those who arrive in our country without proper papers. I am sure you understand that—"

The ranchero waved his large hand and raised his voice again. "Enough! I want this fine man out of your . . ." he wrinkled his nose in disgust, "your accommodations this instant."

"But certainly," agreed Zuniga. "You will accept personal responsibility for his whereabouts and behavior?"

"Yes, yes," snapped Don Pedro. "Bring my horses around now!"

Outside the gate of the presidio, Don Pedro's angry flush had faded and he spoke apologetically to Will.

"I cannot begin to express my sorrow at your treatment, Señor Reed. What must you think of our manners to take such a heroic gentleman as yourself and throw you into such a . . . such a . . . hole?"

The two men were riding side by side, Will mounted on the handsome gray. "The capitan's hospitality was less than cordial," he agreed, "but I've been treated worse. If he was just following orders, I guess it wasn't his fault."

"Ha!" snorted Don Pedro, the anger welling up again. "He's up to something, that one. Currying favor with his commanding general, no doubt."

"Your pardon, señor, but are you a military man yourself? You sit your horse like one, and a magnificent beast he is too."

Don Pedro's smile expressed his approval of Will's judgment. "You have an eye for horses and horsemen, eh young man? Yes, I am retired from the army. I received my land and El Negro here as recompense for my years of service. But the young officers today . . ." He gave a contemptuous gesture with his free hand.

"And how is your son?" inquired Will.

"Out of danger, God be praised. You will see for yourself soon."

"We are returning to the mission then?"

"No, no. You are going to be the honored guest of my humble home. Ricardo was allowed to come home and is anxious to express his gratitude. But now, tell me about yourself."

The two horses kept up an easy, slow canter that covered the ground in a fluid motion. Will related his experiences since joining the trapping party, the ambush, and his time with the Yokuts.

"That reminds me, señor," said Will, interrupting his story. "I came from the Sierras with a mission Indian named Paco, but he disappeared when the grizzly attacked. Do you know him?"

"Paco is a knave and a coward. You are fortunate he did not murder you in your sleep. Give him no more thought. He certainly ran away to save his own skin. If he appears, he shall receive the flogging he so richly deserves."

Don Pedro cast an appraising eye over Will's riding form. "You ride very well. What do you think of Flotada?"

"Flotada? Oh, 'massage'? Do you call him that because of his gentle rocking movement?"

Don Pedro laughed, a deep, resonant laugh that bounced off the green peaks and echoed through the oaks. "Now, yes! But you should have seen him when he was an uneducated brute. We called him Flotada because he *bucked so hard*!"

"My congratulations," offered Will. "He is well-mannered now and a real looker."

"He should be, young man. Flotada is a true son of Andalusian Tordas, the Spanish grays. And," the ranchero paused, "he is yours."

CHAPTER 18

"This is your 'humble' home?" exclaimed Will at the first sight of Don Pedro's rancho. "It is magnificent!"

A flock of pigeons swirled like a cloud of white and gray smoke at the riders' approach. The whitewashed two-story adobe building was nearly eighty feet across its porticoed front. A veranda completely encircled the home, matched by a second-story balcony.

A trio of Indian servants ran to meet the returning ranchero and his guest. Two of them accepted the reins of El Negro and Flotado, while the third, bowing low first, led the way up to the main entrance.

Outside the front door was a bench. Don Pedro sat down, the servant kneeling in front of him. At Will's curious glance, he smiled and explained, "The floors in my home are polished oak. My dear wife, God rest her soul, made me promise to never wear my spurs into the house."

He gestured at Will's moccasin-encased feet. "You do not have that need at present; however, we will soon have you outfitted properly."

Don Pedro led the way. An enormously tall clock with a polished brass pendulum the size and shape of a banjo graced the entryway.

The ranchero gestured toward a formal parlor as

they passed it. "My family and servants would all like to meet you, but first Ricardo wishes to thank you. He is confined to his bed upstairs."

The hallway terminated in a broad, elegant staircase leading up to the second floor. Dressed in his travel-worn buckskins, Will felt even more out of place here than at the mission.

Don Pedro brought him to the second doorway at the right of the stairs. Propped up in an oversized four-poster bed was Ricardo. His head was swathed in bandages and his color looked faded.

Seeing Will, he raised a hand in greeting. An attempted smile only brought pain to the already stretched skin of his face.

"You will pardon me, señor, if I cannot rise to greet you," murmured Ricardo. "The good Father Sanchez, who is the only doctor we have in Santa Barbara, forbids me to move about yet."

"Señor, think nothing of it. To have met oso pardo face-to-face and live to tell of it! Your grandchildren will beg to hear this story over and over," commented Will.

"Yes, head-to-head even," corrected Ricardo ruefully. "And the living here to tell of it is solely due to your intervention."

Will shuffled his moccasins awkwardly. "God let our paths cross at just that instant, so your thanks are due to Him. Had you been armed and I the one attacked, you would have done the same for me."

Then to forestall any further expressions of gratitude, Will asked for more details about the young ranchero's recuperation.

"The good padre stitched my scalp back so tightly that I fear I may look more like a citizen of Cathay than of Mexico. He assures me that all will be well in time, even my left ear, which he at first despaired of saving."

Don Pedro, who had been listening from the doorway, added that Will's speedy actions had saved Ricardo's manly good looks as well as his life. "If he is to make me a grandfather, it is well if the young ladies do not run away in terror when he approaches."

Turning to Will, he added, "Ricardo must rest now, but we would like you to remain as our guest for as long as you wish. The room next to this is prepared for your use and . . . you may wish . . . you will find . . . There are some articles of clothing which should fit you," he concluded delicately.

Will looked from father to son and saw the same expectantly hopeful expression. "It would be my great pleasure to be your guest," he agreed.

"Good!" said Don Pedro, clapping his hands. He regretted his enthusiasm a second later when he saw Ricardo wince at the sudden loud noise. "Shh," he instructed unnecessarily. "Ricardo needs quiet for a time."

The two men closed the door as they exited the room. "Would you care to join me in the parlor in an hour's time?" asked the ranchero. At Will's agreement, he showed the trapper to the guestroom, then turned and went downstairs.

The room was the equal of Ricardo's. There was a finely made walnut armoire and matching dresser and a bed with a feather mattress that looked three feet thick. Trying to recall the last time he had slept on a bed, Will concluded that nothing he had ever slept on deserved to be called a bed compared to this. "Hope I don't drown in it," he chuckled to himself.

Neatly laid out across the silk coverlet was not just

one set of clothing but multiple sets—dress pants, silk shirts, stylish jackets, undergarments. Will wondered what the correct dress was and if he could figure out what went with what. He determined to locate Don Pedro and ask for advice.

Opening the door to find his way downstairs, he bumped headlong into a young woman carrying a bowl and a pitcher of water. In the momentary jostle that followed, Will ended up catching the pitcher just before its contents went on the floor. "Excuse me," he said in English, then changing to Spanish, "I mean, pardon!"

The girl, dressed in a dark red skirt and a white scooped-neck blouse, had shining dark hair that fell softly to the middle of her neck and over smoothly rounded shoulders.

Completely caught off guard, Will lapsed again into English and stammered, "Say, you're really something!"

"Cómo, señor?" returned the girl, appearing not to understand.

Will watched as a rosy glow spread up the señorita's throat to her cheeks. Her complexion, like a fine porcelain cup held up to a firelight, set off her lovely dark eyes.

Finally collecting himself, Will said in Spanish, "No harm done, señorita. No need to be embarrassed. Were you bringing these for me?"

"Si, Señor," she murmured demurely, looking down at the floor.

"Gracias," said Will, taking the bowl from the girl. "Would you tell your master that I'd like his advice on proper dress?"

A curious expression flashed through the young woman's eyes as she looked quickly at Will's face and then away. She pointed toward a complete suit hanging over a chair in the corner of the room. "Not necessary, señor. Perhaps that one there?"

"Ah. Yes. Just right," mumbled Will as the girl departed.

Will dressed in his new California splendor. But he found his thoughts drifting to the beautiful maid of the Rivera household.

The white serge pants went on underneath. The second pair were of heavier dark green wool. They buttoned with silver barrel buttons down the outside of each leg. Will had seen Don Pedro wearing something similar and knew that the overbritches were left unbuttoned below the knee so that the white trouser legs would show.

A finely woven white linen shirt was intended to be worn under a short dark green jacket. The jacket also sported silver clasps to match the pants, but Will had noticed the clasps were left open.

White linen stockings and glove-soft buckskin boots accompanied the outfit. Also included was a flat-crowned, stiff-brimmed black hat trimmed with a horse-hair hat band braided with silver beads. Will elected to omit the hat until something could be done with his hair: it would never fit under the crown now.

Shaved, smelling of lilac water and dressed in the fanciest apparel he'd ever touched, Will cautiously admired himself in the mirror. Around the high collar of the white shirt he knotted a black cravat. The last time he had worn a necktie had been at his uncle's funeral in Vicksburg.

Taken altogether, not half bad, he thought. *I guess that maidservant will approve.* He heard the clock in the downstairs hall strike the hour. *Now to see if the rest of the household agrees.*

Stepping onto the landing at the head of the stairs, Will saw Don Pedro awaiting him at the bottom. "Bueno, Señor Reed," encouraged the ranchero, "you look splendid. Please come along and meet my family."

The sitting room was already filled with people. Seated in the middle of the group was a gray-haired woman with a rather prim expression. She was introduced as Aunt Doña Eulalia. The household matriarch inspected Will closely before suggesting her approval by extending her hand.

Gathered around her chair were the household servants, the head foreman of the rancho and several godchildren of Don Pedro. Each acknowledged the introduction with a bow or curtsy of respect as protocol demanded for the savior of the heir.

When the formal introductions were completed, everyone seemed to relax, until Don Pedro remembered, "Where is Francesca? Why isn't she here?"

From the hallway behind Will a lilting female voice announced, "I'm over here, Father. Everyone was in such a hurry to meet Señor Reed that I was left to put up my hair by myself."

At the first sound of her voice, Will had been startled, then embarrassed. He had mistaken her for a servant! Now it was his turn to feel the heat of a flush rising in his cheeks as he tried to recall their exchange. What had he said? Had he been too forward? Was she offended?

Dressed in fine lace instead of the simple skirt and blouse worn earlier, Francesca entered the room adjusting a lace mantilla on a high comb. She looked the part of a Spanish princess. Her eyes seemed to have a mocking quality as they locked with Will's, as if to say, *The tables are turned now, aren't they?*

But she said nothing to give away the game. Advancing directly toward Will, she offered her hand in greeting, then called to the others, "All right now. Introductions are complete. Must we be so stiff?"

Taking the tongue-tied Will by the arm, she guided an instantly chattering throng into the dining room. Bustling servants soon laid on a feast of monumental proportions.

A steaming tureen of sopa de carne seca y arroz was placed before Doña Eulalia, who stood at one end of the table opposite Don Pedro. Will and Francesca were across from each other in the middle of each side, flanked by the god-children.

Don Pedro recited a blessing over the food, then all were seated. When the tureen's cover was raised, the tantalizing aroma of spicy jerky and rice soup, filled the air. Doña Eulalia tasted the first portion, then allowed a maid to ladle a serving into each diner's bowl.

Will found himself staring down into the soup bowl, looking for the courage to raise his face to Francesca's. Since no inspiration came, he occupied himself by taking several mouthfuls of the soup. It was not until the fourth swallow that the chili seasoning took effect, causing Will to grab for his water glass.

He was afraid he had shamed himself again, until he heard Don Pedro praise the mixture by declaring, "Whew! This broth is capable of raising the dead! Pass the tortillas and the water!"

Roast lamb accompanied by beans, corn, and tortillas was seasoned by the spice of conversation. Everyone wanted to know Will's history and to hear his stories.

The children exclaimed over the tales of Will's wilderness wanderings and Indian ambushes. They all complimented him on his mastery of Spanish.

Finally gathering enough courage to look at Francesca, Will found that she appeared genuinely friendly and interested, with no trace of mocking. She said sincerely, "You may protest that it was Providence which brought you to meet the grizzly, but it was your decision to face the bear when you could have thought only of yourself. Gracias, Señor Reed, thank you."

"In two weeks," announced Don Pedro, "we will have a fiesta and invite all our neighbors to share in honoring Señor Reed." Excited squeals broke out from the younger children around the table.

After dinner, Will managed to find a moment alone with Francesca. "I want to apologize," he said quietly, "for mistaking you for a—for a servant, I mean."

"Doña Eulalia would have scolded *me* for not correcting you at once," she replied with a sincere smile. Offering her smooth white hand to Will again, Francesca said politely, "Let us say no more about it." Then she left Will with the memory of her hand in his.

CHAPTER 19

"Most esteemed Don Pedro," began Don Dominguez.

Such formal speech coming from a neighbor, thought Don Pedro, *I wonder what is coming next?*

"For some time I have given careful consideration to a matter of great importance," continued Dominguez, "and I have decided that the time is correct for me to approach you."

"Go on," said Don Pedro cautiously.

"We are not getting any younger, you and I."

"This is most certainly true," agreed the ranchero. "Do you have a way to prevent it? Perhaps you have discovered a spring of magic water on your property such as the Indios say exists near the Paso de Robles?"

Don Dominguez looked offended at the jesting tone of his neighbor's reply. He ran his hands through his hair as if straightening his ruffled dignity before speaking again.

"As you are aware, I have no son, no heir to my estate. I am, alas, childless," he continued.

Aware that this matter was a difficult and socially delicate one for any ranchero, Don Pedro at once became properly subdued.

"You, yourself," Don Dominguez resumed, "almost

147

lost, most tragically, the staff of your old age, Don Ricardo."

Don Pedro nodded his great bald head and felt again the stab of terror he had experienced when first hearing about Ricardo's injury. Dominguez had gained his complete attention.

"Fate has played with your future in a most devilish fashion. First, your lovely daughter loses her betrothed almost on the eve of her wedding, then you lost your sainted wife, and now almost your son. Do you not see how Providence has preserved you from the misery of Job?"

"I *am* very much aware of how blessed I am that I *still* have two strong, healthy children."

"Is it possible you have missed the divine warning within this blessing? Certainly you see that you must take steps to secure the future, even as I have?"

"What steps exactly?"

"I have decided to adopt Capitan Zuniga as my son and heir, and I would like to announce this important decision at your fiesta."

"I congratulate you. You are certainly welcome to make this announcement at our festivities, but wouldn't you prefer to hold one of your own for the purpose?"

Dominguez smiled at Don Pedro; a slow, easy smile that he must have practiced for days. "But for the second announcement, this would be the proper procedure."

"What second announcement?"

Speaking very carefully, Don Dominguez explained, "Times are very uncertain, are they not? The Mexican government, if it can be called such, changes almost daily, except in its disregard for us Californianos. We must be prepared to take charge of our own destiny."

Don Pedro looked surprised. "You wish to make a political speech at my fiesta?" he demanded.

"No, no!" corrected Dominguez. "You misunderstand me. My point is that you have been most understandably protective of your daughter. But it is time for you to secure her future and yours. My good friend and soon-to-be heir, Capitan Zuniga, has asked me to petition you for the hand of your daughter in marriage."

Don Pedro's first reaction was to be offended at what struck him as a very presumptuous proposal. But on second thought, maybe it made a thread of sense. Zuniga was a strong, though not especially likeable man, and was of a suitable age to marry Francesca. Though not a landowner, if the officer were Dominguez's heir, he would inherit sizable holdings. Moreover, some Rivera property bordered on Dominguez's rancho and if something should happen to Ricardo, while he was unmarried, at least Francesca could retain the land.

"I will not give you an answer at the present, but I will think on this matter," concluded Don Pedro.

"Gracias, Don Pedro. That is all I ask."

Chapter 20

"Quiet, here he comes now," cautioned Don Dominguez to Father Quintana. "Do you understand what to do?"

"Perfectly," assured the little priest.

The two plotters were seated on a low adobe wall that edged the plaza of Pueblo Santa Barbara. They had chosen their location well: just around the corner from the cantina where Don Pedro liked to enjoy a pot of hot, dark chocolate after an early morning ride into town.

Seeing the ranchero arrive and drop off his horse at the livery stable, the two had ample time to secure their position. Don Pedro was seated at his favorite table near the plaza and already sipping his favorite beverage when they began to speak.

In a voice just loud enough to carry to Don Pedro's ears, Dominguez began, "I just don't know what to do, Father."

"I am certain that you will do what is right, my son," soothed the padre.

"Yes, but which is correct? To carry a tale which may be only malicious rumor, or to warn my neighbor against what may be a snake in the grass?"

Don Pedro's ears had by now identified their voices and pricked up at the word "neighbor."

"Tell me all the particulars. Perhaps I can assist you in making up your mind. Rest assured, I will tell no one."

"I do not want to slander anyone, Father, you know that."

"Rest easy, Don Jose, tell me the worst."

"It concerns this American, this Will Reed. As you know, Father, he came here overland as a trader in furs . . . a so-called mountain man."

"Yes, my son, go on," encouraged Father Quintana. Don Pedro was thinking the same thing.

"It has been reported to me that this is a bloodthirsty man who has killed before and will undoubtedly kill again."

Quintana made light of the accusation. "But surely he has fought his way through territory held by savages. One must not judge—"

"Yes, Father, but there is more. He lived for a long time with the Indios . . . like the Indios. He has had Indian wives, and more than one, indulging in heathen and perverted customs I cannot speak of."

"Is this true, Don Dominguez? Can it be proven?"

"Oh no, Father. I heard it from . . . well, no matter . . . another wayfarer, who had no reason to lie. But tell me, Father, what would be best to do?" Dominguez stood, brushed off the seat of his dark blue trousers, and straightened his hat. Quintana stretched as he stood and smoothed out his coarse gray robe.

Though Don Pedro strained his ears, he could not make out any more of the conversation as the two men strolled off across the dusty, sunlit plaza.

He was still sitting, leaning his hand on one work-thickened palm, ten minutes later. A waiter finally stopped by to ask if the chocolate was unsatisfactory.

Don Pedro peered into his cup with as much distaste as if it contained vinegar. "No," he said, "nothing is satisfactory this morning."

———————

From the window of his study, Don Pedro watched as his daughter strolled slowly across the courtyard with the big trapper, Will Reed. The two were engaged in a lively conversation, a fact which did not altogether please him. They walked like two people more interested in each other than in where they were going. Neither seemed to notice the flowers that bloomed on the trellis and lined the adobe-tiled path. Nor did they look up at the blue sky and admire the clear, cloudless weather. No. Each looked only at the other as they walked aimlessly.

Sunlight glinted on the raven black hair of Francesca as if to illuminate the vast difference between her and the copper-haired mountain man. They were a world apart: separate cultures, vastly different lives, different religions. So what was it about this Yankee that so animated the face of Don Pedro's daughter?

He frowned as he considered the question. Perhaps it was those differences that interested Francesca. Yes, that must be the explanation. The very things that drew Francesca to Will Reed now would certainly cause her great heartache if the friendship developed into anything more. She would be better with one of her own kind. Perhaps a man like Captain Zuniga?

At that moment the trapper said something amusing and Francesca burst into laughter. She was enjoying herself far too much.

Don Pedro rocked up on his toes in a gesture that signified his displeasure. Why did she not have a chaperon? Where was Doña Eulalia, who should have been walking within earshot of the couple?

"Doña Eulalia!" Don Pedro called his sister, but he did not leave his place at the window.

His eyes widened as Francesca stooped to pluck a bright orange poppy which she then tucked behind the ear of Will Reed. More laughter!

Once again, Don Pedro called the delinquent aunt. This time it was a bellow, raising the clatter of footsteps on the stair behind him. *She'd better be here in a hurry*, he thought irritably. As Francesca's chaperon, Doña Eulalia had failed today and he would find out why.

A timid knock sounded at his door. Don Pedro called his permission to enter, but instead of his sister it was her servant girl who appeared.

He turned from his watch to glower momentarily at the poor girl. "Where is your mistress?"

"She sent me to say she is ill. She begs your pardon." The girl's hands trembled as did her voice. It was rare for Don Pedro to raise his voice in the house.

"Then you will have to do," Don Pedro said grimly. "Go tell Francesca I wish to speak with her alone. Now!"

The servant nodded, then hesitated. "Francesca . . ."

"She is in the courtyard," Don Pedro gestured out the window as if to give the frightened woman every clue as to his displeasure. "Go! Tell her to come to my study!"

Francesca' eyes were bright with amusement as she considered the poppy in Will Reed's hair. "I have often been amazed when a horse has been left to run the back pastures for a season, how much time it takes to get it presentable for riding. You have curried and combed out nicely for one so long in the mountains."

"I take it that is a compliment of sorts?"

"Proper tack. A good bridle and saddle. A few hours pulling the burrs from the mane. These help the appearance of a horse, but do not always mean he adapts to civilization."

Will smiled and shrugged. "I have not always worn moccasins, you know. It's just that man and beast must' adapt to their surroundings or perish."

"They say you are as much an Indian as the Indians." She turned from him as if she suddenly noticed the flowers and had to stop and consider them.

"In some ways they are as civilized as you or I."

She whirled around. "I differ with you in that opinion. They are ignorant and godless and—"

"Ignorant of the ways of the white man, but like the wild horses, they know the tracks and trails of their world better than you imagine. To them, you might be considered ignorant, Francesca."

She tossed her hair as a mare might toss its mane. She did not like his reply. "They have no knowledge of God . . . or of the church."

At this, he did not argue. He looked thoughtfully at the sky as a blackbird sailed across it. He smiled slightly as though he remembered something . . . *someone*. . . . "You are right in some ways," he conceded. "Death is imponderable to them. They have no real idea of what will come after this life." He shrugged. "But they are just as much eternal souls as you and I. Just as valuable to God as a mission priest, ranchero or ranchero's daughter."

"What do you mean?" she shot back, genuinely offended at his thinly veiled accusation. "That is why there are missions here."

"Jesus Christ was never brutal, never physically cruel. I have heard enough reports about some mission Indians to know that . . ."

Their conversation was cut short by the servant of Doña Eulalia who cleared her throat nervously behind them.

Both Will and Francesca turned to stare at her a moment before she found the courage to speak.

"Your father wishes a word with you, señorita," she ventured, looking toward the study window that framed the figure of Don Pedro. Francesca spotted her father, flushed, and then looked away. He had been watching them.

"Perhaps we shall continue our conversation later, Will Reed," she said in a suddenly cool tone. And then she brushed past him, hurried across the courtyard and into the house.

———

Her father's silence was ominous as he paced the length of his study. His hands were clasped behind his back; a posture he assumed when he was constructing decrees that must be obeyed the moment he pronounced them. Francesca wondered what she might have done to stir his displeasure.

Finally, Don Pedro spoke. "This Americano is not one of us." His opening words were like the death knell rung out by the mission bell after someone died. There was no mistaking the somber meaning.

"No, Father." She said what was necessary and required. Understanding the deeper meaning of his statement, she pretended only to hear the truth that Will Reed was quite different than anyone in California.

"You were talking with him." A stinging accusation, intimating that whatever they were talking about could not be entirely proper.

"About the Indians, Father."

Don Pedro frowned. Everyone knew of the immoral and inhuman practices of the Indians. Was the trapper speaking of the unspeakable to his innocent daughter? "What of the Indios?" he snorted.

Francesca phrased the discussion lightly. "Señor Reed would have made a dedicated priest, Father."

Don Pedro's expression betrayed his surprise. "What is that?"

"He has simply said all the things Mother used to say about them: that they are also eternal souls."

"Who. . . ?"

Her father was wading through his confusion, and Francesca was intent on keeping him away from his reason for calling her.

"Yes," she continued. "Señor Reed is convinced of the great value of the savages, Father. You must talk with him on the matter sometime. Almost word for word the things Mother used to say." She did not mention that Will had spoken of the brutality of the missions against many of the native population. Now was a time to be careful as she related her conversation with Will. If she wished to speak again with him, then she must walk softly through the maze of her father's disapproval.

"I should enjoy hearing his opinion, Francesca, but—"

She interrupted what she knew he was about to say. "Yes. I thought you might enjoy hearing his viewpoint. It is good for the mind to at least look at the ways of those who are so very . . . different from us." She did not add that often one found that there were not as many differences as one thought. "Perhaps after dinner then. You and Ricardo will enjoy his company. I have other things to attend to this afternoon, so I cannot join you. My day to teach the children." She rose and kissed her father on the cheek.

Don Pedro inhaled and looked around the room as if he was trying to locate his lost objections. What was it he was going to forbid her to do? What had he been so angry about?

"You cannot join us for luncheon?" He looked confused.

"I will eat at the mission. You know how the children look forward to their lessons. I cannot be late."

"So much like your mother," he muttered and kissed her on the top of her head. He now was certain his worries were unfounded. Francesca was too bright to fall in love with an outsider; too ingrained with the qualities of her own culture to seek for any fulfillment outside it.

She slipped out of the study unscathed and without any fatherly decrees ringing in her ears. *There is still some hope,* she thought as she changed her clothes. Her father might see the Yankee was not so different as he thought!

CHAPTER 21

"What is the urgency of this meeting and what secrecy requires my arrival at this ungodly hour?" complained Captain Zuniga to Don Dominguez.

"Quiet down," observed the ranchero. "My servants may be awakened by the noise you are making. They may gossip all they wish among themselves, but I do not want them carrying tales to others."

"What tales? What others?"

"Something new has come up. Something that makes it more important than ever for Figueroa to favor *us* and for our other—uh—business to be more productive than ever."

"What can be so new about raising cattle? Have you figured a way to grow a second hide on a steer? Now *that* would be news," sneered the little captain.

The burly ranchero pulled himself up haughtily. "I have a mind to dismiss you and keep this all to myself."

The soldier knew that Dominguez never joked where greed was concerned and he was suddenly all ears. "Your pardon, Don Dominguez," he said. "What is the nature of your news?"

Somewhat pacified by the change in Zuniga's tone, the ranchero explained, "Yesterday a vaquero of mine chased some steers up Canyon Perdido. Last winter's rains caused a mudslide there that uncovered a dark-red rock face. The vaquero did not recognize the ore, but he thought it unusual enough to bring me a sample." Dominguez handed over a lump of rock.

"So?" questioned Zuniga. "It obviously is not gold or silver. This may be the land of precious metals in old fables, Don Dominguez, but California will never produce wealth from the earth."

"Ah, but you are wrong, my good capitan," asserted the ranchero. "This sample is cinnabar, the source of quicksilver."

The captain was all attention now. "Quicksilver? You mean the liquid metal used to refine silver and gold?"

"The very same," asserted Dominguez with finality. "Quicksilver grasps hold of silver and gold as eagerly as you or I. It is used to free the precious metals from the baser elements. Then the quicksilver can be burned away, leaving the wealth behind."

"So it is almost as valuable as gold?" asked Zuniga with a barely controlled squeak in his voice.

"At the moment, even more so. The gold and silver mines of Mexico are dependent on quicksilver from the state of Jalisco—"

"Which is now in turmoil because of the revolutions sweeping Mexico," noted Zuniga.

"Exactly," agreed Don Dominguez. "If we can produce quicksilver in quantity, every would-be ruler of Mexico will want us for his allies. We need not be content with a rancho in Santa Barbara. Oh no! We may soon control California!

"Capitan, I am going to need your help more than ever before. Cinnabar mining will require many workers and the preparation of the quicksilver is hazardous as well. We will need more Indios than ever, only not for Sonora; we will need them here!"

"And the location of the mine?" Zuniga was sure there was more to this. "It is on your own property?"

"By no means! That is why the secrecy is more important than ever. Canyon Perdido is divided between the holdings of the mission and those of Rancho Rivera!"

"And what of the vaquero? What if he should wonder aloud to someone who might know what the ore is?"

The ranchero laid his fleshy chin into his palm in thought. "It would be wise to avoid unnecessary complications. I will have Juan and Iago arrange for him to meet a most unfortunate accident."

"But of course, Don Dominguez." Zuniga's eyes hardened until he gave a good impression of a snake.

CHAPTER 22

"You like this Señor Reed." Francesca's aunt began her remarks without any preamble. She had called her niece into the parlor of the hacienda without any explanation. Francesca only expected the usual discussion of some problem with the servants or a complaint about an inferior grade of lard.

"What? What did you say, Aunt?" Francesca feigned incomprehension to cover her confusion.

"It is all right, child. Did you think that to another woman, even one my age, the signs would not be plain?"

Francesca shook her head and swallowed hard. "But Father would never . . ." she began, trying her best to sound dutiful.

Her aunt patted the needlepoint-decorated stool drawn up near her knees. "Sit here, child. Your father is exactly the subject I wish to speak with you about."

Doña Eulalia inclined her gray-haired head a moment and listened to the sounds of the house. It was midmorning and the servants' duties took them all outside for the time. She nodded to herself in satisfaction that she and Francesca would not be overheard.

"Your father loves you very much and wants your best. Never doubt that. But he cannot replace the advice

163

your mother would have given you. Neither can I, but I must do my best.

"What I wish to say is this: I too loved a young man once, a common sailor. 'Not suitable,' my father said." The old woman's voice dropped.

Francesca waited patiently, then impulsively reached out to her aunt's nervously fidgeting fingers. Doña Eulalia and her niece clasped hands.

At last she found her voice again. "I made plans to run away with him. My father—your grandfather—found out. He had my sailor abducted and sent away on a galleon. I never saw him again.

"So," said the aunt, drawing both her figure and her voice erect. "What lesson is here? Be obedient, child. Be extremely careful to obey your father's wishes. Do not encourage Señor Reed. Be distant, cool, reserved, and, if need be, rude to your young man."

Francesca looked puzzled. "But that is exactly what Father wishes for me . . . Rude? . . . Oh! Yes, I see," she brightened. "I must be very obedient!"

Doña Eulalia chuckled a deep, throaty chuckle in which Francesca caught a fleeting glimpse of a young, headstrong girl who had loved deeply. "Just beware of looking into Señor Reed's green eyes!" she instructed. "Even I find it difficult to be properly reserved!"

In five days time, Ricardo was out of bed despite Padre Sanchez's admonitions. "My friend," the young ranchero said warmly to Will, "I feel fine. Never better, in fact. If I am to properly celebrate at the fiesta in your honor, I must get back on my feet."

Dressed for riding, but with a sombrero two sizes

larger than normal to fit his bandages, Ricardo led the way to the barn. Ricardo's bay horse and the gray Flotada were saddled and awaiting them. They met Francesca coming out of the barn. Will touched his hat brim and started to speak, but Francesca turned her face from him and walked away.

"My father tells me that you ride well," commented Ricardo as Will stared after her a moment, then adjusted the stirrups and tightened the cinch.

"What? Oh, I spent some time on Cumberland ponies back home," acknowledged Will, "and when I came west, I found some pretty fair mountain horses; traded for them with the Crow and the Pawnee."

Will led the gray around the enclosure three times, then stopped to tighten the cinch again.

"Ah," observed Ricardo, repeating Will's actions with his own horse, "I see you are a true vaquero, who knows the paso de la muerte."

"The step of death? Oh, I get your drift," responded Will, climbing aboard Flotada. "I once had a real cinchbinder of a trail horse almost come over with me because I forgot to circle him after tightening the girth. I won't forget that lesson."

The two caballeros rode out together. Ricardo wore a rust-colored suit of velvet and Will was dressed in his dark green.

"Mi amigo, it feels good to be on horseback again," admitted Ricardo as they moved at a slow canter along the road.

Over two hills the riders turned aside from the road and loped across fields of orange poppies and dark blue lupines. They had no particular destination in mind; it was the joy of riding in the late spring air that beckoned them on.

"What are your future plans, amigo?" inquired Ricardo.

Will had to ponder this question for a time. "I'm not sure," he said at last. "My campañeros of the trail are all gone, along with our gear and furs. Maybe I can find someone to stake me to go back and try again."

"Have you not had enough hardship for one lifetime?" asked Ricardo. "Why not stay here and become a ranchero, or if that does not suit you, a merchant like others of your countrymen?"

Will had heard of the easterners who had come to California by ship. Some had accumulated fabulous wealth and prestige like Henry Fitch, now a trader in Pueblo de Los Angeles. Fitch had married Josefia Carrillo, daughter of a prominent San Diego family.

In the settlement around the presidio and mission of Santa Barbara, there were other easterners. Daniel Call was making a living as a carpenter after having jumped ship from the leaky China trader *Atala* back in 1816.

It was even rumored that Don Jose Maria Alfredo Robinson, born plain Alfred Robinson of Boston, hoped to marry into the de la Guerra family. His Yankee business acumen, if united with the de la Guerra riches and respectability, would create a trading operation of considerable force.

Will wondered how others from the East had been accepted so completely while he was treated with suspicion. Ricardo explained that it was the mode of his arrival that made the difference.

With their coastal network of pueblos and presidios, the Mexican government felt able to control immigration from the sea. But overland was another matter. The ranges of mountains that guarded California on the east had long been considered impassable. Now they had been breached, by energetic and voracious trappers and scouts, Americans from the new United States.

In time trade routes might be established and travel regulated so that the Mexican authorities would relax. But for now there was too much internal turmoil in Mexico to allow foreigners to come and go freely.

"So why don't you Californians develop the trading possibilities yourselves?" asked Will.

"It is not suitable for hidalgos to become merchants," commented Ricardo. His reply was without pretense or snobbery; he was simply stating the facts.

"You see, my friend," the young ranchero continued, "there is an order to the universe. Some men are born to rule and others to be ruled; some to be merchants and others to be craftsmen. The Lord God has made it so."

"But," interrupted Will, "what about the Indians? What is their role?"

"I have given this much thought," replied Ricardo seriously. "The holy fathers believed that the Indios could become gente de razón, by study and observation. But I no longer think this possible. They are too childlike to ever govern their own affairs or reason for themselves. They will remain servants forever."

"Seems to me I've heard that point of view from everyone except the Indians themselves," observed Will, reining Flotada back to a walk.

"Enough of this talk of merchandising. I have a powerful thirst," concluded Ricardo, also slowing the bay. "Let us turn aside here for refreshment."

The cantina Corazón del Diablo was as unimposing as its name was sinister. The Devil's Heart was a low adobe structure from which most of the whitewash had peeled. The weathered bricks slumped as if a good rain would melt the building altogether. The hitching rail outside, to which three horses were already tied, looked more substantial. Will noted that one of the horses was a mare.

Inside the saloon were three customers and the proprietress. An older man was seated at a table by himself. His spurs and leather leggings proclaimed him to be a vaquero.

The other two men leaned on the slanted pine plank that served as a bar. They were dressed in badly stained blanket serapes through which their heads protruded. Their unshaven faces were close together and they were laughing loudly at some private joke.

Just as Will and Ricardo were entering, the taller of the two coarse men at the counter spoke. In a voice meant to carry, he said to his companion, "Ugh! Hey, Juan, don't you hate the smell of cow? And have you noticed how those who herd cattle have the manners of cattle as well?"

The lips of the vaquero in the corner may have tightened at this remark, but he gave no other sign of having heard. He took a sip of his drink and set the glass back down.

Seeing Ricardo and Will, the man called Juan whispered something to his loud friend. The first man downed his drink in one gulp and shook off a restraining hand.

"I hear that to keep the vaquero docile they treat them just like the young of the herds—they make steers of them." At this statement, the short, fat woman behind the counter excused herself, saying she needed to go to her casa for more glasses.

Still the vaquero said nothing, but the provocative play was far from over. Now the loud man sauntered over to stand in front of the vaquero, stopping back from the rickety table and folding his arms across his chest.

"Say, you are a vaquero, a cowherd, aren't you? Tell us if it is true. Are you a toro bravo, or only a poor steer?"

With the last taunt still ringing in his ears, the vaquero threw the remaining contents of his glass into the tormentor's face, jumped to his feet and kicked the table out of the way.

When the loud man uncrossed his arms to wipe his face with one hand, he held a long, thin-blade knife in the other. He dropped into a fighting crouch and began to stalk the cowhand. "You are already as lean as an old steer, but maybe I can still trim you some," he jeered.

The vaquero picked up the three-legged stool on which he had been sitting and held it in front like a shield. The knife-wielder lunged in, drew a sweep of the stool, then jumped to the side, slashing the vaquero's sleeve.

"Say amigo, can't a body drink in peace in these parts?" asked Will mildly.

The loud man did not even glance toward the voice. "Keep out of this," he growled. "It is not your fight."

"Maybe not," admitted Will, "but I think I can see it evened out some." As he moved closer to the fight, Juan moved from the bar to confront this imposing white man.

"I would not involve myself, señor," suggested the fat-lipped one. "This is between Iago and the vaquero." With a smile he also drew a dagger-like blade from under his serape.

Will stopped moving and lifted his palms in a gesture

of agreement and smiled in return. The two combatants continued to circle warily, blood dripping from the vaquero's arm.

The trapper had fixed his gaze on the eyes of the man facing him. Will called over his shoulder to Ricardo, "You know what my uncle taught me about situations like this? He said if a man insists on fighting bare-knuckles, oblige him; if someone gets the drop on you with a rifle, give him what he wants. But," the tautly nerved scout added, "do you know what he said to do if someone pulls a knife?" Will pivoted his shoulders slightly to the left as though turning to see Ricardo's reply.

Halfway through the pivot, he spun sharply back toward the right, his right hand doubled into a fist the size of the head of a sledge hammer. With his arm at its fullest extension, he backhanded his fist solidly against the ear of the man guarding him.

"He said I should break his arms," Will concluded, following up the right by stepping through with his left, flush on the man's nose. The fat-lipped one, already staggered sideways, flew backwards against the bar.

His arms bounced straight up over his head from the force of the impact. The knife jumped out of his hand and landed on the floor behind the bar.

At the sudden commotion, the loud man looked around to see the cause. This was all the vaquero needed. He swung the stool hard toward Iago's face.

Iago recovered to bring the point of his knife up to ward off the blow, but the stool knocked the blade from his hand.

"Things are looking a whole lot more even now," commented Will.

Juan grabbed a bottle from the bar and took a clumsy

swing at the scout's head. Will caught the bottle in mid-descent, turned his back into Juan's rush, and lifting under the man's armpit with his other hand, flipped the cutthroat onto the floor.

Will stepped across the prostrate body with his right leg, keeping Juan's arm on the scout's left side. Dropping to his knees, Will fell onto Juan's chest. At the same instant he bent the man's elbow backwards over his thigh. There was a loud pop and Juan screamed once, then passed out.

Iago had never intended this to be a fair fight, and it was apparent his accomplice had been dispatched. Seeing the grim look on the vaquero's face, the coward bolted out the door.

"Your pardon, señors," apologized the cowboy, dashing past Ricardo and Will in his pursuit of Iago.

The failed assassin had already reached the buckskin mare and untied the reins when the vaquero reached his zebra dun. In an unhurried manner, the cowboy took down his reata and shook out a medium sized loop.

As Iago clambered aboard the saddle and spun the mare to flee, a floating ring of braided cowhide settled over his shoulders. He had time to experience an instant's feeling of escape before the rope reached its end and Iago burst backwards out of the saddle.

"What was that about, anyway?" asked Will, who had followed the men out of the cantina.

The vaquero shrugged, "Quién sabe? Who knows, Señor? Perhaps this one . . ." he gestured toward Iago with the spool of reata now coiled in his hands, "had been drinking bad liquor and it made him crazy."

Will studied the scruffy villain now seated sullenly in the dust and trussed up like a chicken. "I don't know," he wondered aloud, "he seemed bent on picking a fight with you. You sure you don't know him?"

"No, señor," said the old vaquero emphatically. "These are not vaqueros, not even jinetes, riders, I have seen before. They are likely ladrones from the cantinas of Pueblo de Los Angeles, robbers fleeing the law."

The motionless form of Juan had been dragged from Corazón del Diablo and deposited in the dirt next to his partner. He had awakened once since being dragged out, but another scream from the pain of the shattered arm and he promptly passed out again. There was no need to tie him up.

A troop of horsemen headed by Captain Zuniga clattered up to the cantina. Zuniga reined to a sudden stop and threw up his hand to halt his squad of soldiers.

"There was a murder reported here and I . . ." he stopped mid-sentence and looked with surprise from Will and the vaquero who were standing, to the dust-covered prostrate forms of Iago and Juan.

"No, no murder," corrected Will, "an attempted one though. Your arrival is very timely, Capitan. You can relieve us of these two snakes."

"I am in charge here," barked the little captain, fairly launching himself from his horse. "Once again, Americano, I find you involved in suspicious circumstances. How do I know that you are not robbing these caballeros!"

The gray-haired cowboy who was no taller than the captain and even thinner, jumped in front of Will and confronted Zuniga. "These caballeros," he bristled, pointing at the two men groaning in the dirt, "are rateros, criminals! I, Diego Olivera declare it to be so!"

"You watch your tongue, old man, or I will arrest you

and this Americano. Now be quiet while—"

Once again the captain was interrupted. This time it was by the voice of Ricardo, speaking from the door of the cantina. "Capitan Zuniga, I can vouch for what took place here. These two malditos provoked a fight with Señor Olivera and *my good friend* Señor Reed only took part to see that it remained fair."

The captain looked angry at Ricardo's presence, and visibly fought to control his emotions. The result was a hideous half-smile, half-grimace that when added to the scar on his cheek made Zuniga look especially evil.

"Ah, Don Ricardo, I did not see you there," said the captain awkwardly.

"Apparently not," concluded Ricardo. "Now, are you willing to take *my* word for what has happened?"

"Si, of course," mumbled the thwarted officer. Ordering his men to take charge of Juan and Iago, Zuniga turned and announced to the old vaquero and Will that they were free to go.

The cowboy only snorted as a reply and Will shook his head in disgust. As he and Ricardo mounted their horses, Will could not resist calling out, "By the way, Capitan Zuniga, how did you know that a murder had taken place here?"

The soldier snapped rigidly upright as if suddenly ordered to attention, then said woodenly, "The proprietress ran to where we were resting our horses by the stream and said that she feared a murder was *going* to take place. That is what I meant."

A few hundred yards back toward Casa Rivera y Cruz, Will and Ricardo were overtaken by Diego Olivera. "Señors," he called, "wait a moment, please."

They had reined up just under an arch of cottonwood

tree branches that laced together over the roadway. "In the confusion, I did not properly thank you," Diego began.

"Not important," responded Will. "They needed to be taught a lesson and I suspect they got it."

The older man drew himself up proudly in his saddle. "You are both gentlemen and I am but a poor vaquero, and yet I am indebted to you. Please accept from me this token of my debt."

Diego untied a small leather pouch that had been hanging behind his saddle. "I note that you are a fine horseman and your beast is a true caballo bravo. Will you accept from me these spurs, as I see you have none?"

Will glanced at Ricardo, who nodded, silently saying *Do not wound his pride.* Will then smiled amiably and the old vaquero passed over the pouch.

"Should you ever need my service," Diego pledged, "you have only to send. I am employed by Don Jose Dominguez. Vaya con Dios!" He clapped his own spurs to his horse and shot away from the young men, waving a final salute over his shoulder as he went.

The spur that fell from the pouch was made of finely worked silver. Will sat on the veranda of the Rivera hacienda examining the old vaquero's gift.

The engraving on the curving side piece was almost worn smooth from years of service, but the spur retained the soft gleam of high quality metal. The rowel was four inches across and carried twelve blunted points. The broad leather strap that fit over the instep of Will's boot and the twin chains that went underneath showed the care of frequent oiling and polishing.

"Ah, my friend," observed Ricardo as Will tried on the spur, "you look like a Spanish vaquero now—let us see you with the other spur in place."

As Will shook the other spur free of the bag, a lump of rock also fell out. It was a dark red fragment of stone no bigger than the scout's thumb.

He held it up and inquired, "What do you suppose this is?"

"I cannot say. A good luck piece, perhaps?"

"If that's true, then I should return it to Señor Olivera. He may have forgotten it was in there."

Ricardo agreed but added, "Why not wait until the fiesta? Señor Olivera will most certainly attend and you can return it then."

"That's a good idea," Will replied, "and since these spurs are too valuable to use every day, I'll keep them in the bag for now."

Ricardo took a moment to reexamine the rock fragment. "I have seen something like this, but I cannot remember where." Shrugging, he handed it back to Will, who placed it with the spurs in the pouch.

CHAPTER 23

"You seem very quiet this evening, mi amigo," observed Ricardo as he and Will walked through the fig orchard at the rear of the hacienda.

Will stopped and leaned his hand on a slender tree trunk. He studied the silver piping on the seam of his dark blue velvet trousers. Still without answering, he raised the sleeve of the jacket and pulled at the cuff of the white silk shirt.

"Ricardo," he said at last, "do I look like I fit in your society?"

"Most certainly," agreed his friend. "You appear as a true caballero bravo, only bigger and red-haired, of course."

"And do I express myself clearly in your language? Have I butchered too many phrases? Have I done things that are offensive?"

"What is this about?" Ricardo asked slowly. "Has someone been rude to you or critical of your speech? He will have to answer to me!"

Will grimaced, making a face between a frown and a silly grin. "That is the problem. It is not a he, it's a she."

"What?" demanded Ricardo.

"Your sister. Don't misunderstand, she has never been anything but polite. But I fear I have offended her."

"What do you mean?" asked the bewildered ranchero, looking back through the trees to the lighted outline of Francesca's window.

"Ever since a conversation we had ... I meant no disrespect ... I can't even remember what I said ... she has been cool, distant. All we talked about was Indians and—"

"Say no more," instructed Ricardo. "It is not fitting that a gentleman such as yourself has to explain. I am certain you said nothing improper. I will speak with her and if she does not behave better, I will have Father instruct her." The young man strode purposefully back toward the house.

"Wait, Ricardo," Will called after him. "I didn't mean for you ..." but his friend had already reentered the hacienda.

"Father," began Ricardo, bursting into Don Pedro's study, "I wish you to speak with Francesca."

Don Pedro was studying a map of the rancho, planning the location of another watering pond for the cattle. "Eh? What's that?" he said, his thoughts interrupted.

"I have spoken with Francesca about the way she speaks to Señor Reed. She gave me a most disrespectful reply. In fact, in words better suited for a muleskinner, she told me to mind my own business."

The elder ranchero stood and clasped his hands behind his back. "Is your sister too forward with the Americano?" he questioned, concern flitting across his brow.

"On the contrary, she has been rude to him. Señor Reed is a fine gentleman, a brave one who saved my life. He must be made to feel welcome in our home. She fails to uphold the courtesy of the house of Rivera y Cruz."

Don Pedro looked confused. One hand remained clenched behind his back while the other passed over the dome of his head. "Certainly, our hospitality cannot be questioned. Señor Reed is our honored guest. I . . . ah . . . I will speak with her."

Francesca repressed a smile as she watched her father pace the length of his study again. His hands were clasped behind his back; his attitude once again was that of the great Ranchero considering how best to pose his decree.

"Father," Francesca ventured timidly, although she did not feel timid. "I wish you would not pace so. It makes me feel as though I have displeased you in some way."

Don Pedro frowned, continuing his walk down to the window overlooking the courtyard where he had first observed Francesca talking so pleasantly with Will Reed. Had he not paced that day as well?

He slowly turned around to face Francesca. "Daughter, I do not understand your behavior," he said at last. Indeed, the tone of disappointment was inherent in his words.

Francesca opened her eyes wider, pretending her innocence. "Whatever have I done, Father?"

"Ricardo has told me—"

"Ricardo!" she scoffed in mock anger. "What does he know about my affairs?"

Don Pedro held up his hands to silence her, a gesture she meekly obeyed. "Now, now! It is not only Ricardo who has noticed, but I, myself, have observed your behavior."

"My behavior?"

"Coolness. To our guest."

"Guest?"

"To Señor Reed you have been . . ." he frowned and rolled his hands as if to make the right words come forth. "You have been more than cool. . . . You have been rude."

"I? Rude?" She protested, and yet she felt a sense of exhilaration. The days of coyness had paid off! Now, instead of instructing her that she must not speak to the American, her father was about to reprimand her for aloofness and command her to pay more attention to their guest. "But Father, he is a stranger. You said it yourself . . . quite different than us. Whatever is Ricardo talking about?"

"I realize it is difficult at times to be polite to one so . . . unlike us. His manners are . . . American . . . his speech is clumsy, but he is the man who saved your brother's life . . ."

Now it was Francesca's turn. Imitating her father's gesture, she raised her hand slightly. "You need not say more, Father," she replied repentantly. "I was not *aware* . . . that I might be offending him. Or being rude. I will try and do better. Really, Father. I will try and make up for it. I was not thinking of Ricardo or the great debt we owe."

The change in Don Pedro's countenance was marvelous to behold. He beamed. Yes, he had raised Francesca to be a proper hostess no matter how difficult the task. "Your mother would be pleased," he smiled. After kissing him lightly on the cheek, Francesca ran upstairs to bathe and change for supper.

CHAPTER 24

Ricardo enthusiastically described the planned events of the fiesta, explaining in detail the succession of trials of skill and courage that would occupy much of the day.

"And will there be a shooting match at this fiesta?" inquired Will.

"There will be the exercise of the lazadores, the ropers, and games of raya and once and—"

"Do any of those involve shooting?" persisted Will.

Ricardo looked dubious. "I doubt that a contest of firearms is planned. Most of the sports are from horseback and—"

"That'll work," said Will. "I'm a fair hand with a horse, but not even close to your vaqueros with their reatas. If I can get a rifle or a brace of pistols, I may be able to show you people a few things."

"We have nothing suitable in the hacienda," observed Ricardo thoughtfully. "Nothing but an old fowling piece. But I know where we may obtain something for you."

The rowboat beached on the white sand below the little community of Santa Barbara belonged to the *Paratus*. It was left on shore for the use of customers whenever the trading ship was in port.

"Ahoy, Captain Easton," called Ricardo as he and Will rowed toward the ship.

"Who's that?" responded Easton, glancing over the deck rails. "Well, welcome aboard, Señor Ricardo. Come up and introduce me to your friend."

The pair climbed a rope ladder to the teakwood deck of the vessel. The fact that Ricardo was a frequent visitor aboard *Paratus* was evident by the ease of manner with which he and Billy greeted each other.

"And this is obviously the American we've been hearing about from the ladies," acknowledged Easton with a nod in Will's direction. "You're certainly a long ways from home," Easton said in English.

The scout took an immediate liking to the trader's hearty handshake and broad smile.

"En Español, por favor," requested Ricardo.

"But of course," agreed Billy switching back easily to Spanish. "And no pirate dialect today either."

At Will's puzzled look, Ricardo explained that Billy put on a swashbuckling act that appealed to the ladies of Santa Barbara. "He adopts an air of mystery and danger because it's good for business," laughed Ricardo.

"Don't give away all my secrets," requested the pirate-merchant with mock ferocity, "or I'll be forced to cut out your heart and feed it to my pet shark!"

"Actually," said Will, "we are here on business." The scout proceeded to explain his intention of demonstrating a mastery of sharpshooting on the day of the fiesta.

"I think I have just what you are after," responded Billy. "Wait here." He disappeared below-decks for a minute, returning with a walnut case inlaid with teak and mahogany. He presented it, unopened, for both men to see the quality of the workmanship, then raised the lid with an expert salesman's touch.

Inside were a matched pair of dueling pistols. Their half-stocks were made of polished walnut and the octagonal steel barrels gleamed.

"These are .50 caliber, and as you see were made as percussion models, not converted flintlocks."

"They are beauties," agreed Will, hefting one to feel the balance. He drew a bead on a masthead to check the sights. "But too expensive for me, I'm sure."

"Nonsense," said Easton. "Take them as a loan. I'll back you in a gentlemanly wager or two and win enough for you to keep them as a gift."

"You place a great deal of confidence in someone you've never seen shoot," observed the trapper.

"You came cross-country living off the land, didn't you? What better recommendation might I need? Come below and we'll get powder and shot."

Ricardo preferred to remain on deck to watch the white clouds pile up on the peaks behind Santa Barbara. The breeze out of the northwest was refreshing and the earlier ocean calm had been replaced by small, dancing waves.

Easton escorted Will down a companionway, then past stores of trade goods. "We can't take long," he noted. "The way the wind is rising, we may have to slip our cable and run out behind the islands till this blows over."

He stopped in front of a double-locked cupboard. "Heard you lived with the valley Indians for a time," he said in English. "Was anything bothering them?"

"The usual tribal feuds, but I think I know what you're asking about. They had a curious way of talking about their people being 'taken by the West,' but then shutting up tight as a clam. Never figured out what they meant."

Easton's pony-tailed hair bobbed as he nodded his agreement. "I thought as much. I've come across some late-night shipping going on at a little cove north of here . . . and the cargo wasn't hides or tallow."

The trader offered no explanation of his mysterious words. He took a key on a string from around his neck and commented, "Powder's here in the Santa Barbara."

"Santa Barbara? Same name as the mission? Why is it called that?"

Easton regarded Will with a questioning look. "Not up on your Catholic saints, eh? Saint Barbara is the lady in charge of sudden calamity—explosions for instance."

Opening the locker, the trader removed a keg of powder and a sack of lead balls. These he passed to Will, along with a small tin of percussion caps.

Reaching into the back of the locker, Easton moved some more kegs around and came out with a cloth-wrapped package. Will could see several more similar packages. "There's also this," he said.

When unwrapped, the object revealed was a brand-new Hawken rifle. Will whistled sharply between his teeth in admiration.

".50 caliber, same as the pistols," noted Easton. "Only this will carry 350 yards and still knock down a grizzly or a man."

"Maybe I'll win the prize at the fiesta and be able to buy this," said Will.

"Nobody else knows I have it," said Easton, wrapping the gun again. "Let's keep it that way, all right?"

"Whatever you say," agreed Will.

"If you find you need it sooner than that fiesta, you

know where to come," the trader concluded, securing the locker.

"Why would I need it at all?" asked the scout, frowning.

"You just remember what I called the powder magazine and that'll do for now," concluded Easton. "You had best get to shore. I'm going to have to get this ship underway."

————

Sensing a need for more courage than it had taken to face grizzlies or hostile Indians, Will had finally worked up enough nerve to take direct action with Francesca. After supper, he caught her by the elbow and asked if she would care to "walk a piece."

To his surprise, she agreed with no hint of reluctance. Saying that she needed a moment to collect a shawl from her room, she left Will standing by the front door, still stunned. As he waited for her to descend the stairs, the scout didn't see the raised eyebrows of his friend Ricardo and the answering nod of approval from Don Pedro.

The fig orchard was all shades of silver from the light of a full moon, sailing up over the surrounding hills like a brilliantly lit ship cresting a dark wave. When Will politely offered Francesca his arm, he was surprised again by the eagerness with which she accepted it.

For a time they strolled in silence. Will knew what he wanted to say, but was so pleased by his initial success that he did not want to take a chance on ruining it.

"Francesca," he said at last, "I'm afraid I was rude to you and offended you. If so, I'm sorry. I'm a plain-speaker and I value that in others, but I had no right to be critical."

The slim, dark-haired girl noted his earnestness, and answered sincerely, "Say no more, Will Reed. There was no offense for you to apologize for."

A hint of lavender wafting from Francesca electrified Will's senses. "But ... but I sounded abrupt when I spoke about the treatment of the Indians. I did not mean you personally, of course. I meant that their path ... if we want to show them a path ..."

Francesca had turned to stand in front of him. Will's great rough hands engulfed her diminutive smooth ones. Her chin jutted up toward his and there was amusement in the sparkle of moonlight reflected in her eyes.

"Hang it all, Francesca," the scout complained. "Here I claimed what a plain speaker I am, and now I can't get words to even come out of my mouth right!"

She smiled up at him then, a dazzling smile of genuine affection and promise. "I understand that mountain men are men of action and not of words," she said.

CHAPTER 25

Will and Ricardo rode out together to take part in the preparations for the fiesta. In Will's honor, a bull-and-bear fight was to take place.

The bull, a huge cinnamon-red toro bravo, was already pawing up the ground in a corral adjacent to the fiesta grounds. The proud bull tossed his head and charged the fences at the slightest provocation of passers-by. When they jumped hurriedly back, he would clash his four-foot-wide dagger-tipped horns against the posts as if saying *I dare you to step in and fight me.*

Ranchero hands were busy reinforcing the stockade and sprucing up the grandstands from which the high ranking guests would watch the action. The purpose of today's journey into the canyons above Santa Barbara was to procure the other combatant for the contest. Will and Ricardo, accompanied by six vaqueros, were going to capture a grizzly bear *alive.*

Will wasn't sure he approved of this venture, especially when the ideas were coming from a man who had nearly lost the top of his head to the crunch of a bear's jaws. But the vaqueros had made their preparations for the capture as calmly as if securing a half-ton of ferocious fury were an everyday occurrence.

The line of riders began to sweep across a hillside

from a little creek that circled its base up to its crest. Will and Ricardo rode behind to observe, although the young ranchero chaffed at not being in the action. His father had made him promise not to take part; not because of the bear but because he might reinjure his head if thrown from his mount.

The vaquero highest on the hill got the first view of the next arroyo over. He gave a shout of discovery, then a moment later a cry of "la osa" in disappointment.

As they rounded the ridge, Will could see down into the canyon. At the bottom, along a stony creed bed was a large mother bear, accompanied by two cubs. The riders began to whistle and shout and slap their reatas against their leather chapedero leggings.

The mother bear stood erect at the noise and gave a sharp "woof" in alarm. The cubs darted across the creek and into the brush, encouraged by a swat from the mother when one did not move fast enough to suit her. Once the cubs were safely across, she too dropped down and rushed after them.

The riders watched until the trio of grizzlies disappeared over the next ridge to the east. As the vaqueros advanced again, Ricardo explained that it would never do to take back a she-bear, although her ferocity in defense of her cubs might be legendary. To pit a female bear against a male bull—what if the bear should win? "Unthinkable," Ricardo remarked, shaking his head.

Several canyons farther on, a vaquero in the middle of the line called out a warning. He had seen the head and shoulders of a great silver-tip bear rising from a thicket of sugar sumac on the hill opposite them.

A low, marshy area in front of the thicket was an ideal capture ground. Shaking out their tallow-smeared reatas, three of the vaqueros trotted their horses in a wide circle to get behind the bear and drive him down into the open.

The other three, backed by Will and Ricardo, slowly advanced to the edge of the clearing.

When the riders on the slope were in position, they began making noises to move the bear downward. "Hey, oso," they called. "We have come to invite you to a fiesta!"

Will and the others did not have long to wait. A few minutes passed and then a huge, hump-backed oso pardo viejo crashed through the brush.

At the last clump of willows opposite the waiting riders, the grizzly threw up his head and sniffed the air. Clearly he did not like something. He shuffled his feet and swung his head from side to side.

The flapping, yelling sounds coming toward him down the slope were enough to finally convince the great bear to move into the open. Out into the marshy space he swayed, then halted again at the sight of the advancing riders.

Immediately the huge bear stood erect, roaring his defiance. He made an almost human gesture of looking over his shoulder as if plotting an escape, then reckoning himself surrounded, he prepared to do battle.

Six riders advanced cautiously toward him, their mounts betraying nervous excitement by stamping and snorting. The vaqueros tried to close the circle evenly, constricting the circle all around.

The bruin, gray-muzzled and slavering, turned slowly around, judging each rider's approach like a boxer looking for an opening. "El Viejo," one vaquero muttered. The title was repeated by the others: Not just *an* old grizzly but *the* old bear of the mountains. Never captured, never bested in a fight, he had disemboweled a half dozen horses and mauled four men—two of them to death.

At last one of the riders, anxious for the glory of being the first to secure a reata to El Viejo, allowed his palomino to get in advance of the others.

Instantly the great bear charged. The vaquero waited coolly, then cast a perfect loop around the grizzly's neck. Two turns of the braided cord were taken around the horn of the saddle as the palomino reared and spun.

The huge bear sat back on his haunches and resisted the pull of the line. This was expected and was the reason why the reatas were covered in tallow. An oso pardo could pull in a horse and rider like a man landing a fish, unless the cord were greased so the bear could not keep a firm grip.

Two other vaqueros quartered the bear, preparing to add their loops to the capture. But El Viejo had not reached his advanced age by doing the expected. When he found that he could not draw in the horse, he simply turned his massive head to one side and bit through the taut rawhide with a snap.

The grizzly immediately charged the nearer of the approaching riders and this time the panicked vaquero made no attempt to cast a loop. It was all he and his bay horse could do to avoid the bear's rush. Even a miraculous leap to the side did not spare them a rake of El Viejo's claws, lacerating the man's leg and the horse's flank.

But the circle of riders continued to close in. The lazadores, three men of great experience with the reata, timed their approach to arrive together. Two loops were flung to snare the bear's head. His parted jaws closed over one, but the other settled around his neck, choking him.

The third man flung his loop so as to capture El Viejo's front paws. Will rode out to take the place of the man who had been injured.

The scout and the remaining vaquero urged their mounts toward the struggling bear. It was attempting to free itself from the noose around its neck by upward thrusts of its bound paws.

Will and the vaquero watched for an opportunity, then each encircled one of the bear's hind legs with a rawhide loop. With little urging from their riders, the well-trained horses pulled stoutly back on the reatas until the grizzly was stretched out on the ground.

The coil around El Viejo's neck was kept tight enough to choke off his wind; no one dared dismount his horse until the massive beast was unconscious. The mounted men were enough to keep the bear spread-eagled on the marshy ground, but the injured vaquero was busy tending his own leg and his limping horse. So although he had made a promise to his father, Ricardo was called on to get off his horse and secure the bruin's muzzle and paws with stout rawhide straps so that the reatas could be released before the grizzly choked to death.

But just as Ricardo bent to secure a strap around the bear's jaws, the mammoth grizzly lunged! He had been shamming and was not unconscious at all!

The bear brought his bound paws upward toward his muzzle, intending to catch Ricardo's leg between his murderous claws and his ponderous head. Whether it was only instinct or a flicker of motion that caught Will's eye, he never could say. But the American's shout of warning came just in time: The young rancher flung himself backward from the bear's clutches, and landed sprawling in the mud.

All the vaqueros immediately tightened their reatas. This time no one approached the grizzly until a few pokes from a long stick proved him unconscious.

The bear was trussed in three times the normal number of rawhide straps and loaded aboard a bull-hide sled to be dragged back to the hacienda. The wounded man rode double behind another vaquero so that his injured bay could be led carefully homeward.

Everyone noticed and commented on how close Ricardo's escape from this second oso pardo had been: from the sweep of the bear's claws, his boot had been slit from top to heel, just missing shredding the leg within.

CHAPTER 26

The morning of the fiesta, dawn was rosy-tinted over the slopes east of Santa Barbara and the wind unusually serene.

Will was up early, laying out his changes of clothing for the day's events. He had been told that tradition demanded at least three different outfits be worn in the course of the day: Green for the paseo, the parade that would start the festivities; dark red for the afternoon's contests of skill and bravery; black with silver for the evening's grand ball.

Will had donned the forest-colored suit and was attaching the emerald green sash when he remembered the spurs given him by Diego Olivera. The scout had placed the pouch in the top drawer of a night stand.

He pulled apart the drawstring of the bag and upended the contents onto the bed. As the spurs tumbled out, so did the curious lump of red ore. Will wondered again about the rock, then shoved it into his pocket, intending to return the piece to Olivera during the fiesta.

The scout picked up the spurs. He was going to carry them out onto the veranda before putting them on, so that the rowels would not gouge the floors as he walked.

That was when he noticed the blurred spot on one of the shanks. While all the rest gleamed evenly, a jagged outline on one limb surrounded an area that looked smeared with a thumbprint of grease.

Will tried polishing the spot to see if it would come off, but all his rubbing and buffing produced no change in the appearance.

Must have been like that a long time, he thought. *Strange I didn't notice the other day.*

Inspecting the outline of the faded area, another thought struck him. Will reached into his pocket and fished out the chunk of stone.

By the early light coming through the bedroom window, Will studied the spur, turning the dark rock over and over in his hand. At last he found a surface of the stone that looked familiar.

Will fitted the edge of the rock against the blurred area of silver. The outline was a perfect match. *What do you suppose makes that happen?* he wondered.

The scout puzzled over this curiosity for a minute before returning the ore to his pocket and picking up his hat. As he headed downstairs he thought, *Another thing to ask Olivera about his lucky rock.*

———

"How will we know when to release the bear?" asked Iago.

He and Juan maintained a healthy distance between themselves and El Viejo's enclosure. Sometimes the bruin demonstrated his savagery, roaring and tearing at the ground and the bars. But now, as at other times, he was dangerously quiet, waiting to rear up and plunge a raking claw through the fence.

"I will maneuver the Americano right into the gate," answered Captain Zuniga. "One of you must watch from

under the stands and signal the other to open the gate."
He pointed to the darkest corner under the seats. "In the
meantime you must hide there."

"This oso pardo is already very angry. He will crush
the Yankee like an eggshell. But where will he stop?"

"That is not our concern. We can blame whatever
happens on the Indios and be rid of the interfering Señor
Reed at the same time."

Zuniga looked up at the pink streaks lighting up the
eastern sky and at the dark mass of the hulking grizzly.
He rubbed the scar on his cheek thoughtfully. "Yes, it
will all work perfectly. Now go, and be certain you stay
well hidden!" he ordered.

———

Will stood on the veranda of the Rivera hacienda,
watching the bustling activity of the courtyard. Grooms
paid particular attention to their equine charges, currying and brushing the manes and forelocks and tails till
not a single tangle remained. An Indian child of age ten
or twelve made the rounds of all the horses' feet with a
bucket and a brush, polishing the hooves until they
gleamed in the sun.

From the balcony of the hacienda, a vaquero dropped
a weighted reata. He allowed it to twist slowly until all
the kinks had been removed from the braided line, then
coiled it carefully up again.

Francesca came out of a door at the far end of the
house and stood, not noticing Will. She was, he thought,
the most beautiful woman he had ever seen. Her lustrous
dark hair was gathered up on her head and pinned in
place with a high comb. A fine lace shawl draped her
ivory shoulders, while about her neck a silver cross on a

black velvet ribbon sparkled at her throat.

It seemed to Will that all the clattering noises of the courtyard were suddenly replaced by a rushing sound. It reminded him of the sound a swiftly plunging river makes as it echoes out of a mountain gorge. He stood entranced, staring at Francesca as if seeing for the first time the goal for which he had been searching.

CHAPTER 27

Will and Ricardo sat on their ringside seats, which meant staying aboard their horses while watching the roping.

A big Chihuahua steer was loosed into the arena, and a moment later an Indian vaquero, mounted on a line-back dun, raced after him. Four lengths into the corral a loop of reata floated over the animal's head.

The dun set his heels and dug in, even as the roper was completing the second dally of braided rawhide around the high, flat horn. The lazadore expertly flipped the slack out of the reata so that it would not get under his mount's hooves.

An instant later the dark red steer hit the end of the cord and was jerked completely off his feet. The roper, who had carried a length of rawhide pigging string in his teeth, vaulted off the dun. He hogtied the steer before the long-horned animal had even twitched, let alone gotten back to his feet.

Ricardo waved his sombrero and there was a round of "Bravo!" and "Well done!" from most of the other riders. A few sat silently, looking sour.

"What's wrong with those men?" asked Will.

"Pay them no mind," suggested Ricardo, straightening his hat. "There are some who still dislike it that my father has trained Indios as vaqueros, and they are perhaps jealous."

Almost as if overhearing this remark, one of the unimpressed men rode forward into the starting position. As Will watched, the lazadore shook out his reata and tied the end fast to the horn of his saddle.

"I thought you weren't supposed to tie the reata," observed Will.

Ricardo was shaking his head. "It is still done by some. Father won't permit it. He says the impact when the steer hits the end of the line is too hard on the horse unless the cord can slip a little around the dally."

The vaquero in the starting gate glanced over where the Indian lazodore who had just roped was coiling his reata. His scowl gave a clear message: *I'll show you how it's done.*

When the rider nodded, another rangy steer was prodded from the pen and the vaquero went flying after the beast. His sorrel colt was young and eager and fast, and the loop of reata left the roper's hand in only two strides.

But the vaquero's haste proved his undoing. He had made his cast before the steer had settled on a course. At the moment of his throw, the lean, grouchy steer veered in front of the sorrel, almost under the horse's nose.

It was the vaquero's misfortune that his throw was good: the loop settled over the steer's neck even as the startled sorrel spurted *ahead* of the steer. All the frantic yanking and sawing on the bridle by the vaquero had no effect and the horse plunged on until he, not the steer, hit the end of the reata.

There was the sound of bursting rawhide and an exclamation of shock. The hard-tied line and the hard-charging colt combined to snap the saddle and its occupant backwards off the horse.

The vaquero hit the ground with a sickening thud. Then as his mount kicked itself free of the girth, he came within inches of having his head reshaped. The horse raced off, still kicking, across the corral.

The roper picked himself up, slowly. Everything seemed to be working and no bones were broken. Dusting off his leggings, he turned around to retrieve his saddle and the audience burst into laughter: he had split the seat out of his trousers!

Will and Ricardo rode around the side of the corral toward the open field where other contests of riding and roping were being held.

"Do you suppose that last vaquero learned something today?" asked Will.

"Perhaps. But he will not like it that he was bested by an Indian *and* made the fool. He may have learned not to tie his reata, but it will not make him treat the Indians any better."

Will pulled Flotada to a stop and pivoted in his saddle. "Ricardo," he said, "explain something to me. Spain's soldiers were in the New World for three hundred years, and many raised families with Indian wives. If most Mexicans are part Indio themselves, why are they so hard on the California tribes?"

"It is not the amount of Indian blood that matters. A family name that goes back to Castille or Aragon is our source of pride."

Ricardo swung his arm in a sweeping circle around the fiesta grounds. "You see the Indios haul water, stack firewood, drive cattle and tend the fields. We, my father and I, treat them well, but they will never be gente de razón. They are like beasts of burden. Some are more clever than others and trainable, but not ever fully civilized."

"What you mean by 'civilized' might change how you view the Indios, but does that give anyone the right to kill them or make slaves of them?" asked Will.

"Oh no!" exclaimed Ricardo. "Only those who willingly join the mission family have requirements placed on them which they must keep. Slavery is illegal and murder is still murder!"

"I wish I were as certain of that as you," shrugged Will. "The Yokuts were terrified of something to their west, and I don't think it was sharks or whales."

———————

A large, grassy field next to the enclosure for the bull-and-bear combat was the scene for the fiesta. It was bordered on two sides by oak trees that provided shady seating for the onlookers.

Francesca and Doña Eulalia were busy organizing the massive amount of food that would be a major part of the fiesta. The quarters from four entire dressed steers were hanging in cheesecloth over the limbs of an oak.

A barbecue fire presided over by three cooks was already blazing and the first of hundreds of pounds of meat was sizzling on the spits.

"Wasn't that a grand paseo?" observed one of Francesca's god-sisters.

"You can't fool me, Margarita," teased Francesca. "You did not see the parade! You only had eyes for the younger son of Don Alfredo."

The girl being teased blushed until her ears turned

pink. She retaliated by blurting out, "You should not talk, Francesca! I know one who was watching you!"

"Well, what of it?" Francesca countered. "Didn't he look splendid?"

"Oh, yes," agreed the younger girl. "And so masterful with his horsemanship. Aren't you excited to see how well he does in the contests?"

"I wonder what he will choose to wear for the lazo. I don't think his customs require so many changes of clothing."

"Well of course he won't change," responded the girl. "He must wear his field uniform until changing into the dress one for the grand ball."

"Uniform?" puzzled Francesca. "What are you talking about, Margarita?"

"Ah," countered the god-sister. "The question is *who* are you talking about?"

"Girls! Girls!" interrupted Doña Eulalia, clapping her hands. "The guests will be coming around for their midday meal soon and we are not close to ready. Francesca, run and check the pasole to see if it is seasoned properly. Margarita, you come with me. We must speed up the making of the tortillas."

———

Across the field, the contests for lazadores, ropers, and jinetes, or riders, were continuing.

"Trust Flotada," Ricardo was laughing. "He knows what to do even if you do not."

"What is this game called again?" inquired Will.

"It is *once*, you know, eleven. If father would permit, I myself would show you how it is done. But I will be here, applauding!"

Will and the gray horse took up their position at the end of a line of riders waiting a turn to compete. Will held Flotada a little to one side so he could watch the proceedings.

When the course was clear, each rider set out at top speed toward a bare patch of ground about fifty yards away. After reaching the edge of the bare space, each jinete did his utmost to set his mount back on its haunches. The parallel skid marks produced by each animal's hind legs looked like the number eleven; *once.*

A pair of boys too young to take part ran out to measure the length of the skid. Each rider got three chances, the best mark counting for the final competition. The vaquero just ahead of Will moved up and prepared his horse at the starting line.

"*Vámenos!*" he shouted to his white-painted bay. Horse and rider flashed across the ground to the edge of the cleared area. A quick jerk on the reins and the horse seemed to sit down abruptly. A plume of dust obscured the action and then the boys called out "Viente-dos!"

"Twenty-two feet!" exclaimed the rider behind Will. "Aiyee, he will be the winner for certain; my eighteen is outclassed."

Will approached the line with Flotada. A wave of a handkerchief announced that the marks had been smoothed out and the scoring zone was clear. As Ricardo had taught him, Will moved his boots slightly so that the loose chains on each spur made a tiny jingle.

Flotada was immediately alert. He flicked his ears back toward the sound, then forward toward the goal, all attention on the business at hand.

The scout's barest tap of the great rowelled spurs was all Flotada needed to bound forward with a great leap, as if crossing a bottomless canyon. In three strides the gray was already at top speed and running as if his life depended on it.

Will could see the clear space coming up quickly. He knew that he would have to anticipate the edge or they would fly past. He raised himself in his stirrups, preparing to gather his weight on the reins and . . .

Flotada needed no more signal than the shift of weight. His great gray body gathered beneath him, till Will's spurs almost touched the ground on either side. The scout found his face next to the horse's head as they slid.

"*Viente-cinco!*" called the boys as Flotada trotted back to the end of the line.

Some of the competitors who had not passed twenty feet on their first attempt now withdrew, leaving Will and six others.

"Well done, señor," complimented the jinete in front of Will.

"Not since the great days of Diego Olivera has a rider reached twenty-five feet."

"Olivera," asked Will. "Do you know him?"

"*Sí, señor,*" responded the rider. "We both worked for Don Dominguez."

"You mean you no longer work there now, or he does not?" asked Will. "In any case, will he be here today?"

The vaquero's face clouded to a deep frown. "No, señor, he will not be here today," he said sadly, "unless his caballero spirit insists on one last rodeo. He was found, dead, only these two days since."

"Dead!" exclaimed the scout. "How did he die?"

"His throat was slit as he rode night herd, señor, and—"

A flash of sunlight gleamed off the polished side piece of Will's spur. "Those spurs, señor," asked the vaquero, his eyes narrowing, "where did you get them?"

"From Olivera. He gave them to me. Listen, I can't explain right now. Where is Capitan Zuniga?"

Will rode out of the line of competitors and circled the field looking for the captain. He found him by the barbecue fire, talking with Francesca.

"Zuniga!" Will demanded, vaulting from Flotada on a sudden stop that would have won the contest for certain. "Zuniga, Olivera is dead. Have you interrogated those cutthroats to see if they had a third accomplice? What were they after? Why were they hounding the old man?"

The captain had not turned to face the scout for any of these questions. Francesca's eyes widened at the raving torrent from Will, and Zuniga at last slowly turned around.

"You are very rude, Americano," observed Zuniga. "If you wish to discuss police business, I suggest that you come to my office next week." He began to turn away.

"Just a minute," demanded Will, closing his powerful hand around Zuniga's elbow. "Pardon me, Francesca, but the capitan and I need to have a talk."

"Of course," Francesca agreed. "I need to attend to other guests as well."

The captain shook off the restraining hand and warned darkly, "Never touch me again, Americano. And never interrupt my conversation unless you no longer have a use for your own tongue."

Will was not impressed, and stood with his hands on his hips. "I want answers, and I want them now. Who killed Olivera? What are you doing to find out? Who hired those criminals and why were they after Olivera in the cantina?"

The officer smirked with his eyes and puckered his thin face as if he smelled something bad. "You have a lot of questions, Americano. Too many that are none of your business. Just so that you will leave me alone, I will tell you: I don't know who hired those men or why, but perhaps they succeeded after all. They escaped from the presidio three nights ago."

"Escaped!" ground out Will. "How convenient. Left no trail either, I suppose."

"I do not like your tone, Miserio. You will apologize at once."

"Apologize," snorted Will, "I'd sooner—"

Ricardo had followed Will's hasty departure from the contest and now stepped between the two men. "Will," he requested, "no unpleasantness. This day is in your honor, after all. Your pardon, Capitan. We will discuss this with you at a more appropriate time."

Will stood staring into Zuniga's face. The squinted green eyes of the trapper locked with the shark expression of the soldier. At last it was Zuniga who turned and walked away.

CHAPTER 28

Will watched Zuniga saunter off toward the plank tables, which were groaning under the weight of the noon meal. Will noted to whom the officer spoke and his manner, following Zuniga with his eyes as if the captain were a wild animal the trapper was tracking.

"Zuniga is a strong man and bad to cross, my friend," cautioned Ricardo. "And he is not without support from some rancheros because they agree with his toughness toward the Indios."

"It is not strength when a man brutalizes those who cannot defend themselves. And it is not toughness to leave a murder unsolved while two likely killers escape."

"Just so," agreed the young ranchero, "but do not provoke the capitan if you can help it. He has a reputation for dueling to the death."

The trapper turned to his friend and said seriously, "Ricardo, sometimes the quality of a man is just as apparent by his enemies as by his friends. I won't be looking to start a fight today, but Zuniga will bear watching."

"Bueno," agreed Ricardo with seeming relief that the matter was temporarily at rest. "Let us address ourselves to the food. We almost had a victory of yours to celebrate in the once, and now we should fortify ourselves for the afternoon's events."

The pair joined a group of fiesta-goers who were picnicking. Francesca invited Will to sit down while she prepared a plate of food for him. Ricardo was attended to by all three Gonzalez sisters.

———

Captain Zuniga had the appearance of a man strolling in the enclosure of the corral, walking off the midday feast. He wandered around the stockade until he was satisfied that no other fiesta-goers were present.

The officer stopped directly in front of the stands with his back to the platform. He kicked idly at the dirt with the toe of his boot and remarked over his shoulder, "Iago, can you hear me?"

"Si, we hear you," came the whispered reply.

"Get ready!" Zuniga hissed in return. "It won't be long now!"

———

After consuming barbecued beef, beans and tortillas, there were ripe strawberries for dessert. The ladies retired to a nearby tent to rest and change while the men returned to a similar structure provided for them. Will swapped his green suit for one of burgundy trimmed in black leather. He was saving the black suit finished in silver for the grand ball in the evening. He also picked up the wooden case of dueling pistols.

Many of the guests took advantage of the break in the events for a midday siesta. In fact, this idea, combined with the warm sun and hearty fare, so appealed to Ricardo that Will had to remind him that it was time for the shooting exhibition.

"I won't need Flotada to do the shooting for me," he

joked. "I handle this part myself."

When Francesca rejoined them, she linked her arm through Will's and together they led a procession toward the corral. Halfway there, Don Pedro was seen approaching on his flashy black horse and the group stopped to wait for his arrival.

At Don Pedro's side rode Don Jose Dominguez, as grouchy as ever in his tight boots. A deep scowl appeared on his face at the sight of Will and Francesca holding hands.

Francesca's father tossed his hat back on his head and mopped his forehead with a silk handkerchief. He was handsomely dressed, as befitted the host of the fiesta. The rust-colored jacket he wore was trimmed in gold, just the reverse of his gold brocade vest with its rust-red piping.

The flowing tail of the sash that wound around the waist of his trousers carried the tones of burnt orange and gold down into a matching saddle blanket. He and the horse seemed to be made of one piece of workmanship.

"Good day, children," he called cheerfully. "I'm sorry to be late. Don Jose wished to discuss some business with me. Is everything to your liking?"

A chorus of "*Sí, bueno!* Most excellent!" responded to his inquiry.

"And where is this procession going? Surely it is too early for the combat of the great beasts?"

Ricardo left his three doting companions—Consuelo, Juanita and Arcadia—and stepped forward to explain. "We are going to the corral for a contest of marksmanship, Father."

Don Dominguez managed to look even more sour

than before. "I suppose this is a Yankee invention."

"Pleased to make your acquaintance too," said Will, his eyes twinkling.

"Bah! No real man cares for anything but horsemanship," argued Don Jose. "Why not let the Americano try his hand at correr al gallo if he wants to show off?"

"What's this about a rooster?" asked Will, turning to Ricardo.

The young ranchero explained that a live rooster was buried up to its neck in a pile of sand. The object was to gallop past at full speed, lean down from the saddle and pull the fowl out by the head.

"Of course, the Yankee may not have the stomach for our sport," needled Don Jose. "Seems he'd rather play with guns."

"Of course I have the stomach for it," retorted Will. "You can put the pot on to boil right now."

"Boil? Pot? What nonsense is this?"

"To cook the dumplings that go with the chicken, of course!"

Don Jose seethed inside as laughter broke out from the group.

"If this is to be a contest, then there must be a challenger," demanded Ricardo. Facing Don Jose Dominguez, he continued, "Since it is you who issued the challenge, Don Jose, will you ride or do you have a champion to propose?"

Don Jose's smile glittered brittlely. "Capitan Zuniga has already agreed to ride against the Americano," he said. The captain was approaching on his lanky bay.

"To make matters more interesting," continued Dominguez, "I wish to propose that the course be laid out right in front of the gate into the corral."

The strategy behind this suggestion was plain: after leaning out of the saddle to grab the rooster's neck, a rider would have only a split second to sit upright again or risk being smashed against the stockade fence. A timid rider would be distracted by the upcoming obstacle and unable to concentrate.

At this point Don Pedro intervened. "I cannot permit this," he said. "Señor Reed is my guest and has never engaged in this sport before. It is not fitting to put him at such a disadvantage."

"I completely understand," said Zuniga through thinly veiled sarcasm. "I would not wish to embarrass anyone, especially the day's heroic guest . . ."

The scout's response was to step off Flotada without speaking and set to work tightening the girth and checking the bridle. As everyone waited to see what would happen, Will completed his preparations and stepped back aboard the gray. At last he spoke: "The way I was raised, a man who's still talking when he should be getting ready usually loses."

The little officer visibly swayed in his saddle as if the raging anger seen on his face was surging through his body. If he responded at all verbally, he would fall into Will's cleverly worded trap, yet if he stepped down to tighten the bay's cinch, he would be seen as following the American's lead.

Zuniga took the only course which his pride would permit. He urged the bay forward without speaking, as if to say, "What are we waiting for?"

The black rooster protested loudly and violently when two Indians tried to place him in a shallow hole in front of the corral. Dominguez swore at them to hurry up and cursed them for being fools and cowards when the rooster flogged and pecked and clawed them.

At last the two men finished and climbed the fence with twenty other mission Indians to watch the contest. Behind them the captive grizzly snarled and growled, rearing to swat the air. He was answered by the deep bellow of the bull from the enclosure across the corral.

The rooster, now buried to his neck, was silent, but his eyes darted around wildly. He pecked furiously at the ground as if he could make it release him.

"The passes will continue until one rider is successful, or until the other is unwilling or unable to continue," declared Ricardo. "Now, who shall go first?"

"Capitan Zuniga," blurted out Don Jose, before anyone else could speak.

Zuniga then settled his hat back on his head. He urged his horse toward the rooster with a sudden jab of his spurs that made the bay spurt forward.

The captain leaned far to the left out of the saddle. Holding his body parallel to the ground, his shark eyes fixed on the rooster's head.

The bay horse ran true and Zuniga's small fingers were closing over the rooster's neck when the captain glanced ahead at the fast approaching stockade fence. He jerked upright in the saddle, pulling the horse up just inside the gate. In his left hand he clutched nothing but air. The rooster was still buried in the sand.

At Will's touch of the spurs, Flotada leapt forward. The scout leaned even farther from the saddle than Zuniga, his fingers almost brushing the ground as he and the horse flew over it. He hooked the rowell of a spur in the girth. The American trusted the horse to run straight and true without any correction from his rider.

Nearer to the rooster they swept and closer to the

corral fence. Flotada corrected his path, moved nearer in line with the target, then straightened out again.

The wall loomed up. Will's hand was open and on course with the rooster. His fingers closed, grasped, pulled—the scout's body snapped upright just before Flotada thundered through the corral gate.

Will looked down at his hand to discover that he clutched feathers. The rooster, even more wild-eyed, was still buried in the sand. Will trotted Flotada back to the watching group. Some of the Indians hopped off the stockade and fanned out to watch the next attempt.

Zuniga spent longer preparing for this run. The little captain tightened the girth on the bay and checked the straps of his spurs. When he mounted again, he nervously shifted his weight, testing the cinch.

As the bay sprinted down the course again, Zuniga hooked the spur of his right foot onto the saddle horn. His body hung downward alongside the horse with his head almost touching the ground.

The horse raced across the space and the officer's hand closed over the rooster's neck. His grip and the surging power of the bay combined to pull the flapping chicken free of the sand.

Zuniga's free hand reached up to grasp the saddle-horn to pull himself back upright. He began a triumphant swing of the rooster so that all could see that he had not missed again; that he was, indeed, the winner.

With Zuniga halfway back into the saddle, the bay horse shrieked an alarm. It plunged to a sudden stop that jolted the officer's handhold loose. Next it reared, flipping Zuniga's spur off the horn and plunging him to the ground. The black rooster squawked and fluttered free.

The horse screamed again, terrified, as El Viejo, the

massive, humpbacked grizzly, confronted him in the middle of the corral gate. The trumpet of fright was cut off mid-shriek as the lumbering grizzly smashed a blow to the bay's head, breaking the horse's neck.

"El Viejo! Oso pardo! The grizzly is loose!" Shouts erupted from the crowd, and the people scattered in confusion like a frightened nest of ants.

Will's first reaction was get Francesca to safety. At a tiny signal from the scout, Flotada whirled and raced toward her. As Will leaned from the saddle, the vagrant thought flashed through his mind that he had warmed up for this necessity only a few moments before.

Gesturing for the girl to lift her arms, Will leaned from the saddle and swept her up behind him without stopping. Flotada sped to the corner of the stockade where the high posts were occupied by Indians who had scrambled up to safety.

Will handed Francesca up. He shouted to them to keep her safe. One of them replied, "We will protect her!"

Spinning the gray around, Will took the reata from the horn and shook out a loop. Other vaqueros were racing in toward the great bear from all around the rodeo grounds.

The first of the lazadores was already flinging his loop at the grizzly. El Viejo stood erect, roaring his defiance and slashing the air with his great claws.

Will saw Zuniga scramble out of harm's way and leap up to scale the stockade. From the speed of his escape, the wiry officer appeared unharmed.

El Viejo took the coil of ungreased reata that had settled around his neck and pulled it toward him. The horse at the other end of the cord was jerked sideways and gave a panicked neigh. The vaquero was forced to draw a knife and slash downward, parting the line.

The grizzly dropped to all fours and charged. Two more vaqueros dashed in to try to distract the bear. He took no notice and pursued the first horse and rider, rising from his crouching lunge to slash at the horse's hindquarters.

Without the greased rawhide cords, the vaqueros were in great jeopardy from the enraged bear. With his terrific power and cunning, he could keep pulling in hapless riders. The ropers who had charged to recapture him only a moment earlier, now drew back a safe distance from the snarling El Viejo.

Sensing the reluctance of his human opponents, El Viejo rushed toward a knot of riders, scattering them. He was headed back toward the wild canyons where he lived, intent on escaping, and not willing for any interference.

In line with his escape was the feasting area of the fiesta, and a group of terrified women and children. The grizzly was aimed straight at them.

Will shouted to Ricardo, "Slow him down some, any way you can!" Urging Flotada to his greatest speed, the scout galloped back to where the case of dueling pistols sat abandoned in the dust.

The pistols had already been loaded in readiness for the marksmanship exhibition. Will knew that the demonstration he was about to give went way beyond what he had planned.

The American thrust one pistol in the sash around his waist and the other he held in readiness. Flotada reversed direction, running flat out down the track of the grizzly.

Ricardo and the other vaqueros were having no success distracting the bear. No matter how they charged at him or made futile casts with their reatas, El Viejo never swerved or slowed except to bite through a lasso and force a threatened lazodore to abandon one.

Will pushed Flotada to overcome the horse's natural instinct for safety and run in close along the bear's flank. The stout-hearted gray obliged and soon the pair had overtaken the grizzly from behind.

Will leveled the pistol at a spot toward the back of the bear's skull and cocked the hammer. Even though the explosion of the pistol followed the click of the hammer by only a second, it was enough warning for El Viejo to swerve toward the horse.

Flotada jerked to the side and spurted past the bear as Will's shot clipped the grizzly's ear and creased his head.

One shot left and only thirty yards before the bear reached women and children too petrified to run. The scout and the gray horse raced ahead of the bear, crossed in front of him, and stopped directly in his path.

Shooting downward at the bear was risky at best because the shot could glance off the bear's ponderous skull. The trapper jumped from the horse and slapped Flotada out of the way.

Will dropped the discharged pistol and drew the other from his sash. He cocked it and drew a bead on the bear. It only took a count of two for the range to close and Will fired.

The lead ball entered the grizzly's gaping mouth as he roared his charge. In what was the best shot the young trapper ever made, the bullet pierced the bear's throat and tore out the back of his skull.

El Viejo's rampage turned into a crashing roll like a

giant furry cannonball bouncing along the ground. The bear's carcass smashed into Will, bowling him over. The scout ended up half under the dead grizzly. One great paw was flung across the man's chest in the appearance of amiable companionship.

Captain Zuniga was yelling something as he jumped down from his perch on the corral. Will was struggling to get out from the monster's weight and could not hear what was said, but he could see the officer waving his arms and gesturing for his squad of solders to join him.

At Will's whistle Flotada rejoined him and the scout remounted as Ricardo rode up. "What has got Zuniga all worked up?" asked Will.

"He says that the Indians let El Viejo out on purpose. He is mad! He is yelling that they were trying to kill him."

————

"Now what?" fumed Dominguez. "You looked like a fool who needed to be rescued, and the Americano is now a hero to everyone, not just the Riveras."

Zuniga's eyes went cold and his hand closed over the hilt of the dagger he carried in his sash. Not surprisingly, the complaints from the blustering ranchero stopped abruptly. "May I remind you," hissed the officer in tones that left no doubt about his willingness to enforce respect by a knife thrust, "that I was the one nearly killed today? What happened to those idiots in the corral? I will cut off their hands and feet after I gouge out their eyes!"

Dominguez, who believed the captain would do exactly what he said, tried to shunt the officer's wrath aside. "Yes, they *are* fools! They claimed the gate did not open when they pulled and then sprang open by itself! But don't destroy them now, not tonight! We still need to move cargo while everyone is preoccupied with the dancing."

Zuniga thrust the half-drawn dagger back into the red velvet sash. "All right," he said, "but after the cargo and the Americano are both disposed of, they are mine to deal with."

Don Jose Dominguez was happy to agree.

CHAPTER 29

The scent of honeysuckle was on the light breeze that blew down from the hills and wafted into the great tent. Where only a grassy field had been for the daytime events, an enormous canvas pavilion had sprung up to house the fandango.

Will, now dressed in his grand ball outfit of midnight black and silver, was standing outside the tarp by one of the guy-ropes. He watched scores of Indians carry plank sections into the tent and assemble them into a dance floor.

Dear God, he prayed, *how I thank you for sparing my life today. And Francesca's.* At the remembrance of sweeping her into his arms and carrying her to safety, a shiver ran down his backbone. *What if I had not been close enough to save her?* he shuddered. It never occurred to him to marvel that he felt more dread at the prospect of her death than he did his own.

Will was so absorbed in his thoughts that he missed hearing a rustle in the grass behind him. Even when it sounded again, his distracted mind dismissed it as a stray puff of wind stirring the canvas doorflap. From inside the tent came sounds of guitars tuning up for the first dance, the jota.

Will was dazzled by another memory: After his fight

with the grizzly, Francesca had run up to him and thrown her arms around him. Even when she at last pulled back, the girl still gripped his arms and held him locked within the embrace of her eyes. *Never leave me,* her eyes had said. *Never frighten me like this again!*

Another scurrying sound reached the scout's ears. This time there was no mistaking the soft press of furtive human footsteps.

Will whirled around, his hands involuntarily grasping for knife or pistol, neither of which were there. "Who is it?" he demanded. "Speak up!"

"Not so loud," requested an urgent whisper. "Señor Reed, it is me, Paco."

"Paco! Come into the light. What are you doing skulking out there?"

"Shh, Señor Reed! Capitan Zuniga will have me killed if I am discovered!"

The American started to argue, then decided that the fear he heard in the mission Indian's voice was real enough. The scout stepped away from the lighted tent, into the pool of shadow around one of the oak trees. He was soon joined by a flitting shape dimly recognizable as Paco.

Even in the faint light, Paco's clothes were obviously ragged. The Indian's face was gaunt and his eyes were hollow.

"Tell me what this is all about," Will ordered in a low, hoarse voice.

"The grizzly today, señor. It was no accident! I was there, under the stands, I saw it all. It was Zuniga and the ones called Juan and Iago."

The trapper started at the link formed by that trio of names. "Go on," he said.

"They were supposed to kill you, but I fixed the great beast's gate so it would not open when they pulled."

"But why me? I mean, what are those three mixed up in?"

"It is not just the three," corrected Paco. "The fat ranchero Dominguez, he is in this also."

"In what? What do two murderers, the capitan of the presidio and a ranchero have in common?"

"Slaves," murmured Paco. "They are selling captured Indians to Sonoran mines. At first it was mission Indians accused of crimes, but to prevent suspicion—"

"Can you prove this?" demanded Will. "I can't go flinging accusations like this to Don Pedro or someone without proof."

"Prove it yourself, señor. I heard them say that they have cargo to move tonight. If either Zuniga or Dominguez leaves the fandango, follow and see for yourself!"

Francesca tried for the third time to catch Will's eye as they swirled past each other on the dance floor in the motion of the jarabe. Each glance she gave him went unanswered, as the scout always seemed to be looking somewhere else.

Anxiety caused her face to flush and her heart to beat faster. The warmth of the air in the tent made it natural for countless fans to appear, and Francesca covered her dismay behind vigorous waving.

At the end of the music, Francesca moved deliberately to where a square of canvas had been rolled up to admit some of the cool evening breeze. Will turned around once before he discovered where she had gone, then spotted her and maneuvered through the crowd to rejoin her.

"You seem very preoccupied, Will," the girl asked with concern. "Were you perhaps injured by El Viejo after all?"

"No, Francesca, I am all right. It's just—"

At that moment, Don Jose Dominguez, who had been in deep conversation with Zuniga near the doorway of the tent, stepped outside and disappeared. "Excuse me," Will said hurriedly. "I'll explain later, Francesca."

"But Will . . ." the girl blurted out, too late. The scout had already ducked through the tent flap and into the night.

Outside, the air was much cooler and moist with the first tendrils of fog drifting in from the channel. Will circled the canvas, ducking his head and murmuring an apology as he bumped into a pair of lovers kissing in the shadows.

The tracker melted into the sheltering fringe of trees and approached the line where the horses of the guests were picketed. A reata was strung between two trees and secured to them by stout iron rings. This cord formed the temporary hitching rail to which the lead ropes were tied.

Flotada recognized Will's scent and nickered a soft welcome. At the sound, Will froze in the darkness and knelt down so that he would not present a man-shaped outline.

Hoping the horse would remain silent, the scout peered out from behind the sheltering tree trunk toward the line of horses. Midway down the row he saw Dominguez untie his mount and swing aboard to ride off.

Will noted the direction the ranchero had taken and

as soon as Don Jose was out of sight, he followed on Flotada. Will rode bareback, with a hackamore improvised from the lead rope. He did not want the silver fittings on the tack to give him away by their jingle or by a flash in the moonlight.

With his hat pulled low over his face, Will plucked the silver buttons from his jacket and stuffed them into his pocket. The gray horse and the rider dressed all in black moved like a specter over the California countryside.

The ranchero was riding at an easy trot, not hurrying, and Will easily kept pace with him. The scout reined to a stop every so often to listen for a change of direction, but the hoofbeats continued up the coast, angling toward the ocean. Dominguez never gave any sign he suspected that he was being pursued.

———————

It was an hour's ride before the smell of salt spray and the low rumble of the breakers announced that the trail had arrived at the Pacific. Following was suddenly much more difficult as the crunch of the waves on the sand covered the sounds Will had been tracking.

Ahead there was a light. It was above the beach on a promontory that stood higher than the strip of sand. The American knew that no habitation existed in such a place, and his instincts told him this was the destination toward which Dominguez was headed.

Trusting that the noise of the surf would drown out his approach, Will rode around the landward side of the hill. He dismounted in a brushy gully back of the knoll, and left Flotada ground-tied.

When the scout had crept across seventy-five of the

hundred yards that separated him from the building, he heard voices. Loudest and very angry sounding was the ranchero's.

"You fools . . ." Will could make out, ". . . him! Zuniga ought . . ."

The scout had reached the windowless rear of an adobe structure. It looked like one of the hide warehouses in which the rancheros stored cured leather in readiness for shipping. Will removed his boots so that they would not crunch on the gravel, and slipped cautiously around the side of the building.

Now the words of the conversation were clear. "Don't make any mistakes," Dominguez was saying. "This will be the last shipment to Sonora. We'll blame the grizzly attack on the mission Indians and use that excuse to round them up. Once our own mine is operating, we'll be too powerful for anyone to care if we increase our work force with some wild Tulereños."

A mine? thought Will. *And what was that about the Tule people?*

A growly voice that reminded Will of the cutthroat known as Iago asked, "What about the Americano?"

Dominguez replied, "We'll kill him and blame that on the Indians too. In fact, we can take care of Don Pedro and his son the same way!"

So it was true! Indians were being taken as slaves. Whatever else the scheme involved, the certain threat of death now hung over Will, Don Pedro and Ricardo.

Will wondered what his next move should be. He knew that he still could not go back and accuse Dominguez without proof; not as long as Zuniga was the law. The scout strained his ears as the slavers entered the building.

"The schooner will send in the boat when we signal. How many are left in this lot?"

Iago replied to Dominguez's question. "A half dozen after the two that died on the way here. But one that is left is an old man nearly dead, and there is a muchacho who won't be good for much."

Will was very near the opening of the shed. The wooden plank door stood ajar. A heavy beam that had been used to bar the door from the outside lay on the ground. The scout stooped to pick up the near end of the beam. His first thought was to trap the conspirators inside and bar the door.

Silently, Will lifted the heavy timber. The light of the lantern inside the building flashed around as the slavers inspected their captives. Ready to slam the door shut and drop the timber in place, Will raised the bar to waist height.

The back of his neck prickled. He pivoted sharply with the heavy beam and swung it against the adobe of the shed like a housewife swinging a carpet beater.

What he had caught between the oak timber and the wall was not carpet but a man. It was Juan, the desperado whose arm Will had broken in the cantina.

Juan's shattered arm was tied across his chest in a dirty bandanna. From the other hand flew the knife which he had intended to use on Will. The scout thought he heard the man's other arm crack in trying to ward off the unexpected blow, but whatever the damage to his arm, Juan was crushed against the bricks of the warehouse. He collapsed with a moan to the ground.

The scout spun back around and tried to jam the beam against the door. Too late! It crashed outward and Iago and Don Jose tumbled through.

"The Americano," growled Iago, launching himself at Will. There was time to fend off one slash with the beam, then the trapper threw it from him because it was too clumsy and slow. The murderer slipped aside as the timber crashed down.

Will had no blade with him, but he stooped quickly and retrieved one of his boots. Reversing it on his hand, he presented the great rowelled spur toward Iago's face.

Will was grateful that Dominguez was a coward at heart. The fat ranchero hung back in the doorway, content to let his henchman do the fighting and take the risks.

And even without a knife, taking on Will Reed involved some risks. When Iago stepped in and thrust the knife forward, he expected the scout to back up. Instead, Will drove his booted fist up under the blade arm, knocking it aside. He followed this move by raking the spur across Iago's face. Three parallel gouges appeared as if by magic, welling full of blood that was black in the dim light.

"Get him," ordered Dominguez.

Iago circled in front of Will, trying to force the scout out of position and trap the spur hand against the wall. When the American saw what was intended, he snapped his arm up, letting the heavy boot fly, rowell points first, at the cutthroat's eyes.

As the man ducked, the scout stepped quickly toward his assailant and a perfectly timed left cross met Iago's chin. The murderer staggered back, his vision unfocused. The gleam from Iago's dagger showed that he had dropped his knife hand.

Will followed the blow to the chin by stepping through with a right into Iago's chest. Now the man's eyes bulged and he choked for breath.

The red-haired trapper grabbed Iago's arm and knocked the knife from his hand by smashing it against the adobe wall. Just then ten thousand stars fell out of the Santa Barbara sky and hit Will on the head. Or so it seemed to him as he slumped to the ground.

When he came to, his wrists and ankles were bound and his hands and feet were tied together behind his back. His first thought was that Dominguez had joined the fight after all, but he was wrong: it was Zuniga.

While Will was lying face down in the dirt at his feet, the captain explained how Will had followed Dominguez from the fiesta, and he in turn had followed the Americano.

"Why are we wasting time?" demanded Iago, wheezing. "He has killed poor Juan. Let me slit his throat and throw him into the sea!"

Dominguez disagreed. "No, not here. We can still make it look like the work of the Indios. We should load this cargo at once and get away from here." Then a new thought seemed to strike him. "Wait! I have heard that the Americano is a great lover of Indians. What could be more fitting than for us to send him with them. No questions are asked at the mines, and no one ever returns."

Zuniga and Iago gripped the scout's arms and roughly tossed him into the warehouse. The door was shut and barred. Iago was left on guard while the other two went to the beach to signal the boat.

The body Will had landed on grunted, but made no other sound. The scout apologized in Spanish, then switching to Yokuts repeated, "I'm sorry."

"Sequoyah!" piped a thin treble voice.

"Blackbird! No! Is that you?" gasped the American.

"Yes," Blackbird whispered, a sob catching in his throat. "Oh, Will Reed! Grandfather and I were captured while gathering herbs. These awful men forced us to march across the mountains with almost no food and only a little water. We were thrown into this prison two days ago."

"Where is Falcon?" Will asked, trying to peer through the darkness.

"Grandfather is very sick," the boy continued anxiously. "He can barely move or speak. Grandfather. Grandfather. Can you hear me?" There was no response.

CHAPTER 30

Will heard Dominguez and Zuniga returning from the beach. Dominguez was cursing loudly. "That no good . . . He calls himself a capitan! He is a coward, a coward! A little breeze springs up and he must hoist a signal that says 'cannot land.' "

Zuniga was more pragmatic. "He does not want to be caught on a lee shore and get beached here."

"Bah! Now we have to guard these wretches for another day. Iago," Dominguez said testily, "you must stay here. We'll be back tonight."

"And the Americano?" Iago asked, drawing his dagger by way of suggestion.

"No, not now," Dominguez stopped him with a look. Then to the officer he explained, "Zuniga, you and I will use this ride to speak of what is best to do with Señor Reed and with Don Pedro. If we plan this properly, since you are the law, you can name me as executor of Don Pedro's property."

"And guardian of his daughter?"

"Exactly so," the ranchero agreed, "and I in turn can start calling you son-in-law as well as son!"

Hearing this plan, Will struggled with his bonds, but without result. "Blackbird," he whispered, "do you think you can undo these knots with your teeth?"

229

Face down in the darkness, Will could not see the boy's enthusiastic nod of agreement. The boy went to work on the thong that pulled the American's hands down toward his ankles.

It was slow going. Even though Blackbird was not trussed up like Will, his hands were tied behind his back. After working on the knots for several hours in the inky blackness of the adobe building, the length of leather strap finally came undone.

Now Will could sit up and move a little in order to put the bindings on his wrists into a better position for Blackbird to work. "Hurry," he whispered. "If Iago comes in to check on us, we'll never get another chance."

It was nearly daybreak when the rawhide that secured Will's hands was loose enough for him to strip it off. He pulled his wrists free, shaking his hands to restore some feeling to them.

Will had begun to work on the cords holding his feet when he heard a noise outside the shed. There was no way to pretend to still be bound, and even tearing feverishly at the leather, the trapper could not get his ankles untied in time.

He jerked himself upright, falling hard against the adobe brick wall next to the door. Leaning alongside the opening, his muscles coiled like snakes preparing to strike. His hands were clenched for the single, two-handed blow he would have one chance to make.

The door opened, but only a small crack. Then it creaked wider apart, but still no one entered. At last it was pulled all the way open, admitting the dim illumination of predawn, but no one stepped across the threshold. Positioned against the wall, Will could not see where the guard stood. Drops of sweat clung to the scout's forehead as he struggled to keep his body tense.

"Reed," a voice called out in English. "Will Reed, are you in there?"

"Easton!" shouted Will, lurching out from the warehouse. "Thank God it's you. How did you find us?"

"Paco here," said Easton, indicating the mission Indian standing behind him. "He watched Zuniga trailing you and followed him. After you got locked up for the night, he came to fetch me."

"But that's ten miles each way and three trips. How could you do that on foot?"

Paco grinned slyly. "I told you it was forbidden for my people to ride. I did not say we did not know how." He went past Will into the warehouse and with a smirk added, "I will untie the rest."

"And what happened to the guard?" asked Will.

"Iago?" responded Easton. "He never sticks around for a fight unless the two-to-one odds are in his favor. Too bad though. I think he has gone to warn Dominguez. We may be heading into trouble if we go back."

"Not if," Will pointed out sharply. "Don Pedro and Ricardo and . . . Francesca are in danger."

"Thought you'd feel that way," said Easton, tossing Will a burlap-wrapped bundle.

"What's this?" asked Will. When he pulled the twine, a buckskin suit and a new Hawken rifle tumbled out.

"Never met a man who could fight his best in unfamiliar rigging," Easton pointed out.

Paco reemerged from the adobe. "Señor Reed, the Yokuts want to go home. But the old man is very bad. Even if they carry him, I don't think he will make it back to their valley."

"Please, Will Reed," begged Blackbird at Will's side,

"you must help my grandfather."

"Try not to worry, Blackbird, I'll see that he gets tended to." To Easton Will said, "We'll take him to Father Sanchez at the mission."

"Mate, we'll be headed straight into their hands," cautioned Easton.

"No matter," said the grim-faced scout. "It's time to take down the evil in the West."

CHAPTER 31

It was an odd looking procession that rode into Pueblo Santa Barbara. Will in his buckskins rode on Flotada with Blackbird behind him. Billy Easton was riding a mule. Falcon was carried on a travois pulled behind Paco's horse.

The mission Indian looked nervously around as he rode. At the first sign of observers he jumped off the horse and walked alongside.

They reached the mission grounds without incident, but several onlookers witnessed their arrival, including Father Quintana. Blackbird and his grandfather were entrusted to the safety and care of Father Sanchez. Will and Easton mounted again to ride out to Don Pedro's rancho.

As they were leaving the mission compound, they were met by a quick-marching file of twenty soldiers and Captain Zuniga. Zuniga's uniform buttons gleamed in the sun and the feathered plume of his hat waved in the wind. "Halt," he ordered. "Señor Reed, I again place you under arrest." Zuniga was so confident of his authority that he gave only a negligent wave of his gloved hand to order his soldiers to form a line blocking the exit from the square.

"What am I charged with this time, Zuniga?" asked

Will. "Does what I know about you make me a spy?"

"Silence!" shrilled Zuniga. "You are charged with wantonly murdering the man named Juan and with stirring up rebellion among the Indios."

"And how do you explain your dealings in slaves and your intended plot to assassinate Don Pedro Rivera y Cruz?" asked Will pointedly.

"Lies. The ravings of a spy desperate to save himself," retorted Zuniga. "Guards, take him."

"Not so fast there, Capitan," suggested Billy Easton, a Hawken rifle across his saddle bow. "I have seen your warehouse and your human 'cargo' and I confirm what Reed here says is the truth."

"Easton, you are charged with smuggling and trafficking in slaves. Soldiers, seize them both."

"Wait!" shouted the voice of Don Jose Dominguez. He stood on the red-tiled roof of the priest's quarters. Beside him, pointing a rifle at Dominguez' quivering face, was the mission Indian Donato. "They killed Iago! Capitan! Tell your men to give up their weapons or they'll kill me too!"

Atop the roofs around three sides of the square stood fifty stony-featured Indians. Most were armed with bows, but others had firearms.

Zuniga gave an animal-like scream of rage. He raised the pistol he was holding and fired it at Will. The lead ball passed under Will's arm and flattened itself against the courtyard fountain as Will and Easton jumped from their mounts to take cover.

A rifle boomed from the rooftop, then another and another. The whiz of arrows being discharged filled the air with the sound of angry, death-dealing bees. Flotada clattered across the courtyard in confusion. Easton's mule bolted, then struck by a stray bullet, fell over on top of a soldier.

Two of the soldiers went down with arrow wounds. The others took cover behind the adobe watering tank as a rain of arrows and rifle balls pattered around them.

Behind the fountain, Will waited, reserving his fire until Zuniga rose up with a musket. Will's shot crashed into the bricks just below the captain's head, lacerating his face with flying scraps of adobe.

"Stop! You must stop!" shouted Dominguez from the rooftop. He was fearful that the mission Indian Donato would blow his head off at any moment. "Listen to me! It was Zuniga! Zuniga caused this to happen!"

Wildly, aiming through eyes blinded by adobe-dust and anger, Zuniga rose and fired at the roof. His shot pierced Dominguez's throat. The ranchero clutched at his neck even as he toppled from the roof to land with a sickening thud on the pavement below.

Will fired at the same instant, and his shot hit the captain square in the chest. As Zuniga fell, three arrows and two lead balls pierced him, including one fired by his own soldiers.

At that moment, Father Sanchez came out of the mission. His arms upraised, he walked boldly into the center of the square. "Donato," he cried. "Lazario. You others. In the name of Christ, stop this killing at once!" Miraculously, rifles and bows were lowered. No more shots were fired. The revolt of the Indians of Mission Santa Barbara ended almost as soon as it had begun.

———

The group gathered in the parlor of the hacienda of Don Pedro Rivera y Cruz included Will, Billy Easton,

Father Sanchez and Ricardo. Together they were sorting things out.

Will drew a leather pouch from his pocket and out of it dropped the small lump of dark-red stone.

"Cinnabar," exclaimed Don Pedro. "Is that what all this is about?"

"And, Father," added Ricardo, "at last I remember where I have seen such ore before: it comes from the Canyon Perdido, on lands shared by us and the mission."

The little council took in the implications of that thought, then Will asked, "What is going to happen to the mission Indians?"

"They have run away into the hills, but they will return when they find out that they are not going to be punished. The two soldiers who were wounded are recovering, and the only two killed, Dominguez and Zuniga, were guilty of goading the neophytes into rebellion and enslaving both neophytes and valley Indians."

"And what about Father Quintana?" asked Don Pedro.

"He also has fled," reported Sanchez, "and it would be best for him if he never returned."

"What will happen if Governor Figueroa decides to step in?" asked Will.

"I do not think we need to worry about that," suggested Don Pedro. "You see, I have today received notice that I have been appointed the governor's representative."

"That's it then, I guess," said Will. "Tell me, Father, how is Falcon? Is he going to live?"

"Live?" chuckled the chubby priest. "That old man is as tough as bullhide. He has already been telling me what herbs are missing from my medical garden! By the way," Father Sanchez continued, "the child tells me that he and his grandfather want to return here after visiting with their people. It seems that someone has told them about a certain path, and they wish to learn more."

CHAPTER 32

Francesca was standing on the balcony of the hacienda, watching the sun set over the sweeping coast of California. A breath of clean summer breeze twirled her fine dark hair and rustled the pleats of her skirt.

Will and Billy Easton were in the courtyard below, and both looked up at Francesca standing there. "Reed," Easton said, "your place is up there with her, so let's keep this goodbye short."

"Thanks for your help, Billy," said the scout, "and for the use of the Hawken."

"You keep that," Easton said, refusing the weapon Will offered. "Call it a wedding present, since I won't be here for the ceremony."

"Oh? Will you be back this way soon?"

"Doubtful," replied the pirate figure. "Things would be a bit uncomfortable for me around here when people start asking where the Indians got those rifles. Anyway, my job is done."

"What job was that?"

"Looking into the situation here in California for President Andy Jackson. He sent me. I am the American spy."

If you would like to contact the authors,
you may write to them at the following address:

Bodie and Brock Thoene
P.O. Box 542
Glenbrook, NV 89413